CHRISTOS IKONOMOU

Good Will Come
From the Sea

Translated from the Greek by Karen Emmerich

archipelago books

Library of Congress Cataloging-in-Publication Data
Oikonomou, Chrāestos, 1970- author. | Emmerich, Karen, translator.
Good will come from the sea / Christos Ikonomou ;
translated from Greek by Karen Emmerich.
Description: First Archipelago Books edition. |
Brooklyn, NY : Archipelago Books, 2019.
LCCN 2018029482 | ISBN 9781939810212 (pbk.)
LCSH: Oikonomou, Chrāestos, 1970---Translations into English.
LCC PA5638.25.I37 A2 2019 | DDC 889.3/4--dc23
LC record available at https://lccn.loc.gov/2018029482

Archipelago Books
232 3rd Street #A111
Brooklyn, NY 11215
www.archipelagobooks.org

Distributed by Penguin Random House
www.penguinrandomhouse.com

Cover art: Louise Bourgeois

Archipelago is grateful for the Onassis Foundation USA's
generous support of the author tour.

This book was made possible by the New York State Council on the Arts with the
support of Governor Andrew M. Cuomo and the New York State Legislature.

Archipelago Books also gratefully acknowledges the generous support of the
Nimick Forbesway Foundation, the Stavros Niarchos Foundation,
Lannan Foundation, the National Endowment for the Arts,
and the New York City Department of Cultural Affairs.

PRINTED IN CANADA

Good Will Come From the Sea

I'll Swallow Your Dreams

I 'll tell you how it happened. How it happened and how it should've happened. About the blood that was spilled and the blood that should've been spilled. I remember everything, I remember it all. And what I remember is even more than what actually happened.

They'd warned him three times. Not once or twice, three times. Tasos, you prick, this won't end well, you'll see what we have in store for you. Tasoulis, we're going to torch your house, nothing will grow in your fields but ash. We'll slit your kids' throats, fuck your wife up the ass. The third time, they tied him to the hood of his truck and ran him through the car wash. Soap, brushes, industrial dryers, the whole works. He was in the hospital for a week, broken teeth, his body flayed by the brushes and chemicals. Like Manolios in *Christ Recrucified*, just the sight of him turned your stomach. That's when Magda lost her shit and took the kids and ran off to Athens. And she told Tasos that if he did any of what he was planning – because he'd made up his mind to go to the cops and call the stations and plaster it all over the internet – that if he did any of that he'd never see her again, or the kids either. And Tasos said OK, but he still wouldn't let sleeping dogs lie. He kept on running around, making a stink, driving us all up the wall.

The whole island knew Xellinakis was behind it. But no one breathed a word, not us and not the rats, either. Not even later on. No one said a word. Who in their right mind would speak up? It's a regular mafia down here, not that shit you see on TV. Henchmen, guys packing heat, a whole parade of Corleones. You talk, you're done. You raise your head, they blow it off. The only reason I'm telling you now is that it's late at night and no one's listening and the wind just whisks my words away. Otherwise I'd keep my mouth shut, too.

And what was it all for? Nothing, nothing at all. Solidarity groups, consumer networks, cutting out the middleman. Poor Tasos. He had all these dreams, for us to build our own cooperative, to start a farmer's market, to help people, to make things happen that Greece had never seen before, without bosses, without party hardliners, shadiness, or crooked deals. The poor bastard. What a naïve piece of work. From the moment he set foot on the island he started making a stink, trying to organize us and the rats, too. And what did he accomplish? Nothing. A big fat zero. The darkness just swallowed him up. For what? For nothing. For a bunch of scallions and two kilos of tomatoes, as the saying goes. For nothing at all.

The second time, later, after they dragged him over to Apsithia, the whole Athens crowd got on his case, trying to convince him to give it up. We pulled out all the stops to try and bring him to his senses. Three or four guys in ski masks had nabbed him on his way home from the fields, bound his hands and legs, tied a black sack over his head and took him out cruising all night in a motorboat on the lake – by which I mean they were in the motorboat, and they'd tossed Tasos in the water and were dragging him around by a rope. We let loose on him, too, but the stubborn ass wouldn't listen to anyone. He just swore right back, called us slaves, chicken-hearted cowards. How do you guys stand it? he said. How can you stand watching that son of a bitch Xellinakis pimp out the whole island? How can you stand the fact that we can't sell our goods where we live, because that asshole comes and takes it all at half price and ships it to Athens and leaves everyone down here buying tomatoes from Holland and potatoes from Egypt? It's worse than the Middle Ages. Even in the Middle Ages things made more sense. Of course we reminded him that none of us are from here, we're all outsiders, so if the rats are in bed with Xellinakis, what can we do, we're just a handful of people, and son of a bitch or no, at the end of the day he's in charge, that's how the system works. Whoever rolls around in the corn will get eaten by chickens, as the saying goes – and I don't mean chickens like us, I mean real chickens. But Tasos wouldn't budge, didn't care what we said. Just called us slaves, bootlickers, yes-men. And then he brought out a bag of oranges and flopped it on the ground and said, just read that, get a load of what it says. Xellinakis Fruits Ltd., navel oranges, origin South Africa, warning, rind unsuitable for human consumption, preserved with imazalil and thiabendazole. You see what's happening? Our oranges are sitting there rotting in their crates, and that bastard is importing oranges from Africa that are drenched in pesticides. And I'll tell you another thing, too. Okay, say you're right, that's how the system works, there are always going to be wolves making millions off your labor and mine, off the sweat of our brows. Say each of us has come into the world to look after ourselves and only ourselves – I don't believe it, I'll never believe it, but let's just say that's how it is, for the sake of argument. Why shouldn't we change that, to whatever extent we can? Why should we just give in without a fight? Why shouldn't we say to Xellinakis, and to everyone like him, listen up, you've squeezed so many millions out of this place, now each of you has to start giving ten, twenty, thirty thousand a year so we can build reservoirs, so all that rainwater won't go wasted. Or, listen up, Niktaris, how much do you charge for that suite with a view of the volcano? A thousand a night? Fine, from now on you'll put ten percent of your profits every year toward building roads, sidewalks, nursery schools. So we can rebuild the health clinic that got destroyed during the earthquake, and keep a ferry running in winter when the tourist lines shut down, and finish the desaliniza-tion plant and the water treatment plant. No ifs ands or buts, that's how it's going to be. I mean, why do you think all those Chinese and Russians are willing to pay a thousand a night to stay in that suite? You think it's the Jacuzzi or the Greek yogurt at the breakfast bar? No, they fork it over because they step out onto that balcony and the view smacks them right in the face, half the Aegean splayed out on a platter with the volcano there in the middle. Well, if you're going to exploit the island, the island deserves its share, too. You can't just pocket it all. So, Kyria Eleonora, if you're going to sell the sunset at Magou Beach so all those poor suckers will cough up a hundred euros a head to eat farmed sea bream and dentex from Senegal – well, you'll give this much each year for us to put bins on the streets so Minas doesn't have to ride around on his mule picking trash off the cobblestones, like we're stuck in the '60s. That's the deal. You've stripped this island to the bone all these years, you've eaten every last morsel of meat, and now it's time for you to pay up. It's time for you to do something for the island. And since you won't do it on your own, we'll have to force you. Make no mistake, you'll pay. The time has come, it's your turn to pay.

That's the sort of stuff he said, the same bullshit you read online by your average blogger in need of a good lay. And each time, first when they stuck a pistol in his mouth, then when they almost drowned him in the lake, and finally when they drove him through the car wash and he came out looking like a leper – he just kept saying the same shit. But later, too, at Christmas, when that sour-assed Magda left him, took the kids and ran off to Athens and almost didn't come back, he still kept saying the same shit, not even that could knock any sense into him.

The same old shit, right up to the end.

And what was it all for? Nothing. Tomatoes from Holland and grouper from Senegal.

That's the sort of shit that destroyed Tasos – fucking orange peels, imazalil, and thiabendazole.

Solidarity and justice, that's what finally took Tasos. Solidarity and justice – empty words that poor people say, not because they believe in them, but because they're poor.

But none of us could have guessed he'd go the way he did.

We all expected the end to be more manly, more heroic. The kind of thing they'd show afterwards on television and the internet, something that would force those stinking carcasses we call politicians to at least make a statement or two in Parliament. And even now, whenever we go up to the Refuge and look down at the sea from up there, we say he should've chosen some other end, more heroic, more manly. We remember all the crazy shit he used to say, about how good would come from the sea, and we say if he'd done something more heroic and manly, maybe people would have heard and risen up. Maybe something would have happened, something would have changed. I don't know, maybe.

Fairy tales, you'll say. But you know what? People need a good fairy tale every now and then. People invented fairy tales and filled them with monsters so they wouldn't become monsters themselves. Because the truth can turn you into a monster. You have to become a monster if you want to withstand the truth.

Something more heroic and manly, that's what we expected of Tasos. We thought he'd be some kind of Samson, who took others with him when he went, who killed more people in dying than he did while he was alive. That's what we expected. But he betrayed us.

We thought we had a Samson on our hands, but he turned out a Cobain.

Such a betrayal.

Though we all agree that these days, with this country in the gutter, a real man, a hero, isn't the guy who fights evil, but the guy who learns to live with it.

———

The women didn't want to go to the cave. Not to the Refuge, or to any other cave, either. Who ever heard of celebrating Easter in a cave? What are we, cavemen? What if there's another earthquake and the cave comes crashing down on us? That's the sort of stuff they said. I mean, Lena just tossed off a few comments at first, and then calmed down pretty fast. But the others were in full revolution mode. Magda most of all, she was convinced that Tasos had put the rest of us up to it, and wouldn't stop nagging, pecking away at him with her worries. As if she knew. As if she knew what was going to happen. Even if they say you shouldn't believe in signs. Tasos turned a deaf ear, he'd made up his mind and wasn't about to back down. And we weren't, either. Why make such a fuss, we said. It'll be great. And it's the guy's name day, after all, he should get to decide where we celebrate. Besides, the way things are going, sooner or later we'll all be living in caves again. We might as well get some practice.

And we weren't just saying it – we believed it. We believed it, and we still do. All those motherfucking politicians, Greeks and foreigners both, are going to send us back to caveman days. We'll all be living in caves, with clubs and animal skins.

We'll be lucky if we still have fire.

Besides, most of us hadn't celebrated Easter on the island before, and we were all hoping to avoid the rats if we could. It's their custom to celebrate together in the streets and town squares. You know what that means. All year long they stab one another in the back, are at one another's throats, and on Easter they're suddenly one big family. Rats. Of course it's not fair for us to call them that. Not fair to actual rats, I mean – even rats don't pull shit like that. Take Lazaros, the guy they call the Bow, whose son disappeared not too long after Tasos. He's one of us, he has a taverna down in Abyssalos and out back he's got chickens, turkeys, stuff like that. At some point he realized that eggs were going missing from the coop. Must be rats getting in there, he says. And he wracked his brains to figure out how they were stealing eggs without breaking them, but he couldn't make heads or tails of it. So one night he stakes the place out to figure out how they do it. And what does he see? One rat sneaks into the chicken coop and grabs an egg with all four feet at once, then rolls onto its back. Then another rat comes in, bites the first by the tail and drags it out of the coop and back to their nest. See? That's how rats operate in real life. Teamwork. Whereas these guys here are always looking for a chance to screw one another over, and if they ever band together it's only to screw us, instead.

But I'm getting off track, I'd set out to say something else.

There was that whole episode with the baptismal font, too. About a month ago someone stole the font from the church of Saint Yiannis the Warrior, up on the mountain, and they tried to blame it on us. The Athenians took it, they said. The hell we did, we said. What the fuck would we do with a font? Use it as a kiddie pool or something? No, they said, you sold it for the copper. Ten euros per kilo, a hundred-kilo font, that's a clean thousand in your pockets. Well, we said, if we're counting to a thousand, your wives and daughters have probably sucked a thousand dicks this year, you can start there. Fuckers, fucking assholes. Neither side pulled any punches that time, and believe me, things got pretty ugly. First they say we're stealing their jobs, then it's their fields, now they've got us stealing baptismal fucking fonts out of their churches. Hear that, wind? Hear who's talking a big talk about stealing? Those assholes, who for all those years charmed us into coming to these snake-hole islands, and picked our pockets clean at their hotels and tavernas. All those years they stole from us, and now they despise us. That sucker Tasos was right. All these years we've been stealing from Greece and now that the country is ruined we despise it. It's the same with us. Now that we're ruined and there's nothing left for them to steal, they despise us. As if we wanted to leave our homes and come here to the end of God's earth, like Adam in exile. As if we came from another country, as if we weren't all Greeks, all one breed.

Then there was that business with the Germans on Clean Monday. Two summers ago a German TV station came and filmed an hour-long show about us – you can imagine, the Greeks who became migrants in their own country, the Athens of the Aegean, that kind of thing. I don't know how word got out, but pretty soon there were crowds knocking down our doors, TV stations and newspapers from all over the world, film crews, photographers, reporters, overnight Little Athens where we live looked more like Cirque Medrano. And then the Chinese started showing up in droves, and those fags drove poor Elvis crazy, because apparently in China it's good luck to meet someone who survived a shipwreck, and when they learned that Elvis walked away not from one but from three, they went nuts. We're talking hysterics, you've never seen anything like it. There were lines down the street, people waiting for hours just to touch him or ask for his autograph, and all these Chinese girls dressed as brides coming to sit in his lap and swoon and croon and take photographs for good luck. I mean, they even invited him to be the best man at their weddings, we're talking total insanity. Of course it all suited Elvis just fine, since he could grab an ass every now and then, and he was making good money, too – he'd set up a regular donation box like the ones in church, with a price list, and in the evening, when the show was over, he'd go down to the American's place and buy a round for everyone and get wasted on tsikoudia. Things went on that way for a year or so, until one evening in May, not long after the business with Tasos, he was down by the lighthouse and ran into two Chinese girls from a cruise ship who were pretty plastered themselves, and who knows what happened, but at some point everyone in the tavernas along the harbor saw them running by half-naked, screaming and crying, and then they saw Elvis speeding off on his motorbike – and that was that. After that night no one ever saw him again, he just disappeared. We searched everywhere, we turned the whole island upside down, but we didn't even find the motorbike. He vanished into thin air.

First Tasos, then Elvis, then Lazaros's kid. How do people just disappear like that, can you tell me? I don't understand how a person can just disappear.

It's scary, isn't it?

But that's not what I meant to say, either. There was something else I had in mind.

I was talking about the tourists. For two years now we've been the hottest show in town. They stop us in the streets, they come uninvited into our yards and homes, film us and photograph us like we're monkeys at the zoo. We're even in the guidebooks – and the other day there

– 24 –

was another big hullabaloo over in Tourtoura. There's an old campground down there, it's been abandoned for years, and last year a bunch of freaks from Athens broke into the place and occupied it. There were maybe thirty of them, and they put a sign up at the gate that says, "No cops, fascists, tourists, or other urban scum." At first there were a few run-ins with the police, who tried a couple of times to kick them out, because the rats claimed they were coming out at night to steal chickens or take watermelons from the fields, but the kids from Athens had the bright idea of dousing themselves with gasoline and threatening to set themselves on fire, so the cops pussied out and these days they mostly just let them be. We don't have much to do with them, either – they don't bother us, we don't bother them. They just hang out in there, smoking their joints, playing their guitars and their drums, growing their tomatoes, green beans, and hatred for society. That's what they told Tasos once when he got it into his head to talk to them about Xellinakis, suggested they join forces on the cooperative he wanted to start. We just grow whatever we need for ourselves, and that includes our hatred for your society, they said, and sent him packing. Then the other day there was a huge uproar, because some idiots went over there, Norwegians, Swedes, who knows where they were from, and they scaled the wall and started snapping photographs, and the druggie kids came out with bats and started chasing them around. The rats made a big deal of the whole thing, they say we're chasing the tourists away when we should really be grateful for all the free publicity they're giving us all over the world. They brought up that business of Elvis and the Chinese girls and what happened even before that with the Germans and shouted and called us every name you can imagine. Fucking foreigners, they said, screw them and the day they set foot on this island – and they were talking about us, not the tourists.

Now I remember, I was going to tell you about the Germans.

On Clean Monday a couple of our guys took their families down to the harbor to eat at Marika's place. A bunch of Germans are sitting at the next table over, and at some point one of them gets up, piss drunk, and starts snapping pictures. What's up, chief, our guys say, what's there to take pictures of? You've never seen people eating before? So that douchebag of a German turns to them and you know what he says? I'm taking pictures of you, he says, because over at our table we ordered two salads and a couple of beers for all of us, and you guys are eating like the world is ending, and you're eating with our money. You can guess how the rest of the story goes. Our crew had all had a little too much to drink, so they grabbed the German and the rest of his group and practically left them for dead. If the cops hadn't shown up in droves, they'd still be at it. You've never seen anything like it. And those asswipe cops arrested our guys, wanted to lock them up. So all of us Athenians head down to the station and tell the chief of police, you'd better watch what you do, or we'll tear down these walls and you can use this place as a beach bar instead of a jail. In the end they let them go, but those asshole rats got everyone all riled up again, saying we're ruining the island's reputation and sending the tourists away. See what I mean? Instead of doing something about those fuckers who come here and chase us around all day with cameras like we're Mao Mao in the jungle, those bastards just join in the chase.

Slaves to the system, that's what they are. Cowards. Foreigners.

That's what they call us.

Foreigners.

Foreigners, outsiders, refubees. Not refugees, refubees – their little joke down here on the island, like the ones who came in swarms from Asia Minor back in '22.

There's one good thing about all of you descending on us, an old-timer rat once said to Tasos. Thanks to you, we remembered words we'd gone and forgotten.

They call us foreigners. They call us Athenians, too. Even those of us from Piraeus. Not to mention everyone from Larissa and Thessaloniki and Patras – it doesn't matter where you're from, to them we're all Athenians. And the whole neighborhood from the church of Saint Marina down to the Pits, they call it Little Athens. It doesn't matter where we're actually from, to them we're all Athenians. Athenians, refubees, foreigners.

Foreigners.

Us, foreigners.

OK, I know, I got carried away again. But it just gums up the works, throws your mind for a loop, like a gear off its track.

It was the kind of day you think doesn't even exist anymore. I don't know what kind of Easter you guys had up there, but here it was one of those days you think you'll never see again, as if they carted them off along with everything else. You stare at the blue of the sky and feel like crying because you were born with arms instead of wings. Or imagine being able to push a button and explode into a thousand pieces, tiny slivers, and the bits could float off in all directions, up to the peak of Mount War and far out to sea, scattering for whole kilometers, over lakes and streams, orchards, olive groves and vineyards and outcroppings of rock, grazing grounds and forests and slopes covered with scree, over plains, bridges, mills, chapels and monasteries, over lighthouses, harbors, fishing boats, boatyards, over bushes and trees, junipers, myrtles, pine trees, carob trees, oaks, spruce, plane trees, cedars, fir trees, willow trees, beech trees, walnuts and chestnuts – to explode into a thousand pieces, to float off in all directions, because trapped in your tiny body, how could you ever really feel the world? That's the kind of day Easter was here. Even the women calmed down as we climbed up to the Refuge. Twice they wanted to stop and pick flowers and I remember watching them run with the children at the side of the road, laughing and shouting, how their faces shone in the sunlight, how the breeze rustled their hair, how they pulled their skirts up above their knees so they wouldn't get caught on the underbrush, how they straightened the bra straps on their shoulders, how they hugged the children in their arms, how they decorated the girls' hair with daisies and poppies as red as blood, how they looked at us with eyes the color of soil after a rain – I remember us watching and saying that women are the gears that make the Earth turn, and then we said how scary it all was, how scary to struggle to build a life for yourself all over again from the beginning, trying to banish the greatest of all fears, which isn't the fear of death but the fear of life, the fear of living, the fear of living a life in fear, the fear of life that makes us die a little bit every day.

There was a whole caravan of us, forty or so, including the women and children. We and Tasos made seven, then another seven or so with Balsamos and Tremo, Psis and Chryssa, Minas and Yota and the twins. Salamander was there with his daughter Kassia, he still hadn't lost his hair at that point, and Lazaros whose son disappeared after Tasos, and Harmless's widow who has that screwy son in the wheelchair. Rita came, too, the one who opened a pet shop in town last year, and this year built a cemetery for dogs and cats up in Drakiana where all the weirdos go to bury their Irma or Psipsina or Goofy and put photographs on the graves and oil lamps and crosses and even erect headstones, I love you, Ruby, I miss you, sweetheart, Daddy and Mommy will remember you forever – they even bury ducks and turtles and rabbits up there, and Rita gets mad when we tell her she should build a cemetery just for rats, you'll rake it in hand over fist, we say, there are people who can't afford to bury their mothers and fathers and those assholes go and put up marble graves for their cats and guard dogs, fuck their stinking rat town, fuck the whole place. Elvis came, and Midis, the one they call TNT because he blew off his right hand with dynamite, and Stathis the security guard at the asylum, and that blow job Elina with her man – we weren't sure he'd fit in the cave what with all those horns sprouting from his head. The Kombos brothers came, Tomis and that guy Zack, the cripple, and crazy Charonis, who runs a water taxi and in the summer takes tourists out for moonlit rides on his boat, the *Archangel Michael*, and sings them bits of the *Erotokritos* with his lute, and tells them stories in three languages about goblins and dragons and nymphs – it's a regular startup, you wouldn't believe how inventive we foreigners are in opening businesses, trying to make ends meet, I mean, just imagine, an oar, a lute, and dearest Aretousa, have you heard the unhappy tidings? At the very last minute, we convinced old Gougouis to come, a guy in his seventies whose grandkids kicked him out of the house this winter so they could turn it into a bed and breakfast, and Popeye, too, who was stuck under the ruins for two days after the big earthquake on Parnitha and the terror of that time made his eyes bulge out – and when we started getting earthquakes here, too, he dug out an old German helmet of his grandfather's he'd kept from the Occupation, and ever since he wears that thing day and night, just in case the ceiling comes crashing down on his head. There were some newcomers, too – a few couples with no children, the kid from Larissa and the blond girl who both work for that Corleone Theodorakis's cleaning service, Manos who takes care of the plastic frames at the greenhouses and whose wife left him later on, and Ariadne, the constable's widow pushing her baby in the carriage.

All the Athenians came, all the foreigners.

Most of them hadn't ever gone up to the Refuge before, some had never been in a cave in their lives. And that ended up not being their first time, either, because as soon as we got there, the women dug their heels in for good. Some of the men, too. Tasos and Tremo and some others had gone up at dawn to set up the generators and spits and get the fires going. We'd planned on gathering in the cave, in the wide, flat clearing to the right as you enter. That's where we'd set up our picnic, we'd eat there, and drink, and get the celebration going. In the cave. We'd set out lanterns and light fires and when we started dancing our shadows would dance with us, we'd become a hundred, two hundred souls, as if each of us had two shadows. In our drunkenness we'd believe we were an enormous crowd, and take courage in our numbers. We need to practice, we'd say, try it out, get used to it as best we can, because the kingdom of caves is at hand, the time is coming when we'll actually have to go back to living in caves. And then we would gather the bones from the lamb we'd eaten and place them in a dark corner, deep in the cave, so that at some point, centuries later, the people living here then might find them, if there are still people on the planet. By that time maybe they'll have invented some very advanced systems that will tell them we came up to the Refuge that Easter Sunday, at this particular time, we stayed this long, we were this many altogether, this many women, men, and children, we ate this many lambs and this many goats, who knows, maybe they'll be so advanced they'll even be able to see us and hear us, to resurrect our shadows and the echo of our voices, to resurrect the sound of women crying and children laughing, because let's not kid ourselves, some bit of each of us lingers forever in this world, that's why every place on earth is full of the shadows and voices and laughter and crying of the dead, except most of us can't see any of that, or hear it, either, because that's how it should be, that's how the living should be, blind and deaf to the dead, otherwise how could you go on living, you'd go crazy, which is why I think maybe we shouldn't hide those bones after all, because I don't want to think about whether a day will come when the living will be able to see and hear the dead through their laptops and cell phones, Christ himself said it best, let the dead bury the dead, and Christ said that God isn't the God of the dead but the God of the living, though I guess if it's going to happen, it'll happen whether or not we leave any bones to be found, and who are we to decide what the future will bring, what people will be like in fifty or a hundred years, though I still think if the living were less concerned with the dead and more concerned about the people who haven't yet been born, the world might be a better place, or might become a better place, but then again who knows – that's the kind of crazy shit Tasos was spouting, hours later, when we'd drunk the ten-liter cask to the dregs and opened the barrel of strong red wine that Midis brought.

But I've gotten ahead of myself, I lost track again.

When we got up to the Refuge, the women dug in their heels. And fine, they did have a point. There's no denying it's a wilderness, with the cliff and the sea down below, the kind of place that could drive a person mad. They had a point, but then again we were all there together that day, in a crowd big enough that there was nothing to be afraid of. And then that crackpot Charonis starts in on his whole routine. Saying there's a bottomless pit at the very back of the cave and if you get too close it sucks you in and you're gone, and a few years ago they found some tiny skulls in the cave, the skulls of little kids mounted on stakes, and a few years before that some guys raped a tourist in there and then threw her over the cliff, and if you listen closely, you can hear her at night, crying and howling, and a hunter came up here last year and found a baby abandoned outside the cave, and when he got close, the baby started to laugh, and it seemed to have silver teeth, but it was actually hundreds of tiny black worms pouring out of the baby's mouth, and one night some guys came up from Tafia to look for old coins, and when they'd gone pretty deep into the cave they saw something thick and red like blood dripping down onto the rocks from above and one went over and touched it and it burned his hands and then they saw a big fire with soldiers sitting in a circle around it wearing tunics and cartridge belts, with long hair and beards, and they were all soaked in blood from head to toe, and the guys from Tafia clawed their way out of the cave and as soon as they got outside they saw that their watches were all broken and each one showed a different time – Charonis the nut job was on a roll, there was no stopping him. And it wouldn't have been so bad if he'd at least told the stories he tells to the tourists when he takes them out on his moonlit boat rides, stories about the olden days, full of nymphs and princesses and witches with green eyes, instead of stories about the present, stories from last year or the year before or even this year, as if fear had become just another gadget, an iFear that keeps coming out in a new version every time you turn around, endless upgrades, iPhone, iPad, iFear, iFuckYouAll with your cell phones and tablets and ghosts. And the bastard was so convincing that our hair stood on end, as the saying goes. As the saying goes. Anyhow, eventually we settled on a compromise. We wanted to gather in the cave, the women down under the plane trees, and in the end we set up at the mouth of the cave, neither in nor out. But they still couldn't just enjoy themselves. They kept worrying that the kids might sneak into the cave, or wander out towards the cliff, or climb up the trees. And they kept complaining about how we'd made them come all the way up here to the Refuge on Easter, why couldn't we have gone to Abyssalos, to Mahaira, to the Agioupes, or at least down to some beach, Magou, Katergo, Pikroneri. Had they all been wiped off the map or something? What were we doing up there in the middle of nowhere, on a holiday like that? Men with families, what business did we have running around in deserted forests and caves?

They were fixing for a fight, but given what day it was we decided to show our best selves.

Given the day.

———— ∞ ————

We got wasted off the very first drop. I'd guess we were wasted before we even started to drink. The light. That light was to blame, for sure. So white and clean it made your gaze go black. Even in the shade, at the mouth of the cave or under the plane trees, you felt the sunlight wrap itself around you, creeping over you like a living thing struggling to get inside and banish the darkness within. It couldn't, of course. And we just laughed. We laughed as we looked at the blackness of the cave and the hollows in the trees gaping around us like black mouths. We laughed and our laughter echoed in the blackness that surrounded us, in the blackness we had inside.

Tasos pulled his younger kid into his lap.

Kostis, what sound does a chicken make?

Kokoko.

A kitty cat?

Niaouniaou.

And a lamb?

Bzzzzzzzz.

Get it? He'd heard the electric spit rotating and thought that was the sound a lamb makes – bzzzzzzzz. We laughed. We laughed a lot that day. We pinched Kostis's cheeks, mussed his hair. How could we have known. Kids. Supposedly so innocent. I don't buy it. The other day, our kid's teacher, who's as bad a cunt-scratcher as you'll find, asked the class to write something about what food they'd be if they were a food. The kid writes this whole thing about how if he were a food, he'd want to be soup, so poor people and sick people could eat him and get warm. You hear that, wind? Just seven years old, and that's what he wrote. Of course with everything he sees and hears, what else could he write? So the teacher gave him first prize, bravo, Petrakis, you're the best in the class. The next day when school lets out, two or three kids from his class start pushing him around, some little rat kids. Petrakis, we're sick and poor, sit still so we can eat you. And they pinned him down and bit him all over until he was covered with bruises. You hear what the little bastards did? They actually bit him, I swear. In the end they kick him a couple of times and push him into the mud. He comes home soaked in mud and tears, and what do we see? He's black and blue all over with bite-marks, arms, legs, even his back. At first he couldn't even speak, he was trembling like a leaf. I took him in my arms and my whole body shook, too, from his shaking. After a while, he told us what happened. You can imagine how the blood rose to my head. I wanted to go and find those brats and tear them limb from limb. But Lena held me back. She was afraid it might make things worse. We're alone here, she says. We're alone and there are so many of them. We're strangers here, who's going to come to our defense? She was right, of course. The same thoughts have been running through my head day and night ever since we came here. We're alone, we're strangers, who will defend us. And worst of all is the sea. Did you ever think you'd hear a thing like that from me? But it's true. The island is a prison, and the sea is the bars. If you're on the mainland and something happens, you just head for the hills, pack up the car and you're off. But how are you supposed to escape this place? I mean, where can you go? The island is a prison, I'm telling you. For people like us, it's a prison. It took me a while to learn that lesson. But it's true. A prison. They knew a thing or two back in the civil war, when they used to send people into exile on the islands, and during the dictatorship, too. And now we're right back to the same old shit. You'll say we've got democracy now. Sure. Back then they sent people to the islands by force, now we come here on our own. It makes all the difference, right? Right.

In the end I didn't go and try to find those brats. I just played the hen, sat tight on my nest, swallowed my anger. Patience, I said to myself. Patience, this too shall pass.

What sound does Dad make, Petrakis?

Kokoko.

What I told myself then is, if you haven't felt like a coward you won't ever be a man. I believe it. I really do. Before we came here, the thought never crossed my mind. If you haven't felt cowardice, if you don't know how it feels to be afraid to speak out, to shout, to fight, you can't really call yourself a man. And if you've never been betrayed by a woman you aren't a real man, either. But that's another story.

I know, I got distracted again. But I said it before, the gears are off track.

What sound, Petrakis, does Dad make?

Kokoko.

Petrakis, what sound does Dad make?

Kokoko.

What sound does Dad make, Petrakis?

Kokoko.

———

We danced at the mouth of the cave. We danced in a circle that opened and closed and broke off into smaller circles. We all danced, even those of us who didn't know how, and it was as if we were stepping on smoldering coals. We danced holding hands and arms and shoulders – we danced holding children, our kids and other people's kids, we danced with that strange sunlight falling on us and making shadows that weren't black but white, we danced and the light filtered between the leaves and branches of the trees, creating shadows on us like hands, white hands that slid over us and wrapped themselves around us, white hands touching us, touching our wives and our kids. And you'll say I'm sitting here and spouting fairytales about white hands and black mouths, but I told you from the beginning, I'll tell you everything, I remember it all, I remember the things that happened and the things that didn't happen, that might have happened and should have happened, I remember it all, and I'll tell you everything, like it or not.

We danced the tsamiko. We danced the kalamatiano, the balo, the sousta, dances from Epirus, whatever each person knew. Tsiftetelia, zeibekika, hasaposervika. We danced dances no one had ever seen before, dances we made up as we went along. We danced with our eyes closed, stomping our feet on the ground, clapping our hands in the air, and as we danced we remembered parties and celebrations and wild nights from our past, old loves, drunken binges. And we felt our chests constrict, our eyes burn, and we wanted to shout, to cry, to let loose and bring the whole world crashing down, to set it on fire so that nothing was left standing, to turn everything to ash. Tasos had grabbed Psis's pistol and every so often would go off a ways and fire it into the air. The echo made each shot sound like ten. The women and children would clap their hands over their ears in surprise, blinking like hunted animals, like deer in headlights. And Tasos laughed and kept shooting. He loaded the chamber, shot, and laughed, his face ruined by the scars the brushes had left, his teeth broken, a mouthful of dilapidated fence. I hadn't seen him laugh like that in ages. Partly because he didn't like showing his teeth – when they tied him to the hood of his truck and drove him through the car wash the bridge at the front of his mouth had broken and now he was ashamed to laugh. He even lisped a little. That's why he didn't talk all that much anymore. Because he didn't want people to see his teeth, and because of the lisp, too. See? That's the sort of people we've been collecting down here for the past three years. People who are ashamed to laugh. People with broken bridges. People like broken bridges. Broken. Cracked.

People like that.

I don't remember what happened next. I mean, of course I remember, I just don't want to talk about it. I told you, I remember everything. The things that happened and didn't happen and should have happened.

I remember everything. But I'm tired. I'm tired of talking, tired of remembering.

I'm getting cold, too.

It's freezing out here tonight.

What time do you think it is?

Tasos loaded the chamber and shot, loaded and shot. He kept muttering to himself, too. At some point I went over to tell him to watch it, we didn't need any more trouble – if I'd only known – and I heard him talking to himself. Big deal, you'll say. We all do that. All of us foreigners, all of us Athenians talk to ourselves. For starters, we talk all the time – just talk and talk. It's strange. We talk and talk, we babble, wherever we are, to whoever we're with. If there isn't anyone around, we talk to ourselves. We all talk to ourselves. Me too, I'm no exception. You know how often I catch myself in the fields talking to the tomatoes and cucumbers? Some talk to dogs, or cats, or seagulls, others to God or the dead or people they left back at home, wherever they came from. On winter nights people stand at the window, all bundled up, and talk to the darkness. If you weren't a person, if you were the night, say, or the wind, the fire in the fireplace, the smoke rising from that fireplace or from the wood stove – if you were the warmth and smell that rise from burning wood, that warmth that gives you some small hope that all isn't yet lost, a hope you pray won't die out as soon as the wood becomes charcoal, a blackened lump – if you were one of those things, you would hear them talking for hours into the darkness, talking to the lights on the islands across the way or to the passing ships. And now that the weather is a bit better, they go outside at night and talk to the moon, to the stars or wind. One guy talks to the sirocco, another to the north wind. Just like me, right now.

We all talk to ourselves.

Because we can't stand the silence. It's too much to bear.

I know what you'll say. There's no sense in saying it, I already know. You'll say a man should be strong and keep his feelings to himself, that true pain is always silent, that the things that really count can't be expressed in words – I know all that, I know and I agree. But when you live on an island things are different. Here words are a kind of comfort, words seem to lessen the fear. Sometimes I think the first humans learned to talk in order to lessen the fear they felt in the caves where they lived. And here on the island we learned to talk all the time, to ourselves and anything else, in order to lessen the fear we feel in this place where we came to live. The island is our cave. That's why we talk to ourselves. Because silence breeds monsters. Silence makes fear grow.

All of us talk all the time, to ourselves and anything else.

The only ones we don't talk to are the locals, the rats. Nothing beyond the absolutely necessary. What can you say to people like that? Besides, even if you wanted to talk to them, you'd have to find another language. Take the word treehouse. What do we mean when we say treehouse back where we're from? The little houses we used to build up in trees when we were kids, and we'd climb up and pretend they were real. Isn't that what the word means? Well, when they say treehouse down here, they mean the houses they build *for* the trees. Let's say you have a lemon tree and you build a little stone wall around it so the wind doesn't blow it over. The rats call that a treehouse. Now just try and communicate with people like that. And that's just a simple example, right?

A simple example.

There are plenty more.

We swear, too. A lot. Even the women and children, we all swear. You wouldn't believe the kind of shit we talk. Sometimes we joke that we've invented a new language, Shitlish. You know, how we say someone speaks English or Swedish – well, we all speak Shitlish. And I'll tell you something else and you can laugh if you like. Sometimes I think that's the most frightening thing of all. That we curse and swear from morning till night. That we wake up swearing and fall asleep with Shitlish on our tongues. That. Ever since we came here, we've slowly stopped talking the way we think, and now we think the way we talk. I don't know if you get what I'm trying to say. Instead of our minds making up the words, it seems to me that now the words make up our minds. What I mean is, if you get used to calling all women whores and all men assholes and all children brats, you slowly begin to believe that's how it really is – that all women are whores, all men are assholes, all children are brats. And I don't think it makes any difference if you believe that your own wife isn't a whore, or your own kids aren't brats, or you yourself aren't an asshole. No difference at all. Not a bit. Not one bit.

But I got carried away again.

I'd set out to say something else.

So, I'd gone over to Tasos to tell him to rein it in, but there was no need, because as soon as I got there, he handed me the pistol and ran off. He'd sent the kid from Larissa to look through the CDs for a particular song he wanted to hear. As soon as the kid found it and waved the CD at him, Tasos headed like a shot for the dance floor.

This one's mine, he shouted. Out of the way, all of you. This one's mine.

what endless passion
endless
is mine

Have you ever seen, in November or December, when the sirocco is dying down, how the mist dances over the waves at night? How it rises, whirling, and disappears, then later you see it again and then it disappears again, until you think the sirocco is something your eyes have made up? That's how Tasos danced that night. As elusive as mist.

and like the quiet rain
like the rain
my tears flow

I stood and watched from a distance, my finger tickling the trigger. I imagined the gun was a flamethrower, imagined pulling the trigger and watching the whole place light up like the Arkadi Monastery during the Cretan revolt. I must have been about ten sheets to the wind at that point. Meanwhile, everyone else had knelt down and was clapping. Magda, Lena, Yiota, Rita, Chryssa. Elvis, Valsamos, Psis, Tremo – I remember them all. Minas had stripped off his shirt and was pounding his chest like Tarzan, the Salamander was rolling around on the ground, as hammered as they come, Zack almost tipped over his wheelchair – even that nutjob Popeye had taken off his helmet and was bashing his head with it. And the blond who worked for Theodorakis, pretty drunk herself, barefoot, hair loose. The kid from Larissa was watching her from across the way, full of longing.

Ariadne the constable's widow was clapping the baby's hands as it napped against her chest – remind me to tell you her story one day, the hair on your head will stand up straight to the ceiling. I remember them all. And Tasos was dancing with a cigarette burning his lips, elusive, eyes closed, barely moving his feet, as if he were dancing in a minefield and that half meter of land where he stood was the only spot that had been cleared, and if he made even one wrong move a mine would explode and shoot us all sky-high. Then Tomis, Zack's brother, jumps up and fills a glass to the brim and goes over and gives it to him. And Tasos drains it in a single swallow and sets it upside-down on the ground. He spins around and bends down, just touches it lightly with his finger, and the glass shatters into pieces. You've never seen anything like it. He just touched it, like that. Smithereens.

> I'll go and find a cave
> a cave
> with rocks and dirt
> and there I'll leave my bones
> my bones
> my body, life, and soul

How long could the song have lasted? Three minutes? It seemed like three hours. And when it was over, I saw Lena get to her feet, and she turned and looked at me, standing off to the side with the pistol in my hand. She was wearing a short jean skirt and those red boots, and from where I was standing, and as smashed as I was, she looked as if she were soaked in blood up to the knees. She stared at me as if she didn't recognize my face, as if she was struggling to figure out who that guy was, standing there with a pistol in his hand. I remember smiling at her, and then I shoved the pistol in my mouth and pretended to pull the trigger, then took it back out and blew on the barrel. Like that, see? Have you ever done that? Put a loaded gun in your mouth? Bit down on the metal, felt the bitter steel on your tongue? If you do, you'll see what it's like. All sorts of things run through your mind in that moment. All sorts of things.

Then Lena started toward me, but Valsamos headed her off and pulled her over to dance. I stood there and watched her dancing an Epirot dance, and I must have jinxed her by watching – if it's possible to jinx the woman you've been with for ten years – because at some point I see her suddenly teetering to one side, and she almost fell. The heel of her boot had snapped off. And my knees went weak, too, I thought, great, she's probably broken her leg and we'll be running to the hospital. If you can even find a doctor and they don't send you across to Naxos or Syros, and if you can find an x-ray machine, and bandages and casts and all the rest – because as they say, it's not enough that you have a whole hospital on the island, you want doctors and nurses and machines, too? And how is she going to come out to help in the fields with that broken leg? And who's going to look after the kid? All that passed through my mind in an instant. Fortunately it was only the heel, and she barely noticed. She just flung both boots over to the side and kept dancing, barefoot. She grabbed our kid by the hand and they danced together, she showed him the steps. And you should've seen him, he picked it up in no time. As smart as a jackal, that one, just like his mom. And I was flooded with shame. Aren't you ashamed of yourself, I thought, you sorry excuse for a man? Aren't you ashamed of thinking only of yourself? How did you sink so low. What a disgrace. And then I saw her boots tossed to the side of the dance floor and it hit me. I mean, my lord. Look at that, I think. Look how low I've sunk, that I can't even buy her a new pair of boots. And you know how crazy she is about boots. You remember. How I used to buy her two or three pairs each winter. Tall boots, short boots, with heels, without. Expensive ones, real leather, not the cheap kind from the Chinese stores. Not to mention the other shoes, the clothes, the perfumes and skin creams. Plus a new cell phone every time I turned around, and the trips, the vacations. And I held that pistol in my hand and said to myself, I wish it were a flame-thrower, so I could pull the trigger and turn everything to ash. That's what I keep thinking that whole time. If I could just heap everything into a huge pile and burn it, destroy it all. Clothes, shoes, the kid's toys, everything. Watch it all turn to ash, so I wouldn't have to remember any of it anymore. So I wouldn't see all those things and remember how we used to be and what we've become. You might ask, great, say you burn it all, what will that get you? What'll you do after that, go around barefoot, wearing sheepskins? I don't know. I just don't want to remember. I don't want to remember anything.

Sometimes I think, we lost our jobs, our homes, our lives – why can't we lose our memory, too? Why? Why did they take everything else but leave us our memory? Why couldn't they take that, too, while they were at it?

Becoming poor isn't what breaks you. What breaks you is remembering that you didn't used to be poor. That's what breaks you.

Right after that is when Minas collapsed. He was just dancing there, and all of a sudden he fell in a heap as if someone had trimmed off his limbs. Everyone ran over, Yiota grabbed him, shouting for someone to bring water and vinegar and rub his temples. The twins started crying, shaking like poisoned dogs. The women picked them up and took them a little ways off, where they wouldn't see. A man two meters tall, just lopped off like that. His face as white as a sheet, coated in sweat. As if all his blood had become sweat. Something similar had happened a few other times, too. Once we were all there, one evening down at the harbor, at Marika's place. We did everything we could to bring him to his senses. And now it was just the same. He never liked to take pills, even though we've got everything a person could want down here, Xanax, Lexotanil, Zoloft, Ladose, Inderal – take your pick. Sometimes we joke that when we're finally completely broke, we'll just use our pills as

currency. Five kilos of potatoes equals a box of Lexotanil. Ten eggs, two boxes of Xanax. But you had to be
there to understand. A man two meters tall in a heap on
the ground. Yiota bent over him, wetting his hair with
one hand and stroking his cheeks with the other. It was
strange. I don't know, it was strange. Have you ever seen
fish blasted out of the water with dynamite? How their
eyes shine when they float up to the surface? Like fake
fish, as if they were never alive at all. That's how our
eyes looked as we stood around Yiota and Minas, those
were the kinds of eyes we watched them with. And afterward, when he seemed a little better, we carried him to
the car and he and Yiota left – we would take the kids
down later on. And Tasos came over and took the pistol
back and asked if I had anything on me. And I said sure
and we went a little ways off, to that shelter with the
benches they built over the cliff so you can sit and watch
the sunset. I pulled my gear out of my underwear and
rolled us a joint and lit it and we smoked, standing there
together. We stared out at the sea, the sky, the islands
darkening in the distance – Milos, Kimolos, Polivos. I
remember how the sea glittered, the waves a thousand
fragments, but I didn't say anything, because I didn't

want to jinx the moment. Tasos didn't say anything, either. Only at some point, when we were almost done, he said again that good would come from the sea. Good will come from the sea, he said. I don't know why that had stuck in his head, but he said it all the time. And always in the same way, kind of singing, and if you asked, he'd tell you it was a line from a song. None of us knew that song, none of us had ever heard it. But it sure got stuck in our heads, too, and now we say it all the time. Whenever anything goes wrong, whenever any of us gets bad news – be patient, we say, good will come from the sea. Good will come from the sea. It's something we foreigners say, a kind of password just for us.

Good will come from the sea, Tasos said.

Shut up, man, I said. I mean, didn't you hear?

What?

Good broke down, they took it in for repairs. It's going to be a while before they can get it up and running. At least a hundred years, they say.

He looked at me for a minute and then started to laugh, one hand over his mouth, as if he could hide from me. Then, I remember, he stretched his hands out in front of him and looked at them and said, if Christ really was a carpenter, I bet his hands were as covered in marks and scars as mine. Just think how strange it must have been for him to perform all those miracles with hands like that. For him to heal the blind, the paralyzed, lepers, touching them with swollen, crooked fingers. I wish I could do that. Even if I'm no Christ. Or even a carpenter.

Then, out of the blue, he grabbed me around the shoulders and hugged me, and I remember thinking, poor Tasos, what kind of Christ would you be with that face, those teeth, but I didn't say anything, I just let him hug me and then pushed him away and said, what are you feeling me up for, I'm not blind or paralyzed, nothing to heal here.

I know, he said. It's just the drink. Whenever I drink I can't keep my mouth shut.

But he wouldn't let me go. He held my arm and leaned his head on my shoulder and wouldn't let me go. I looked out the corner of my eye at his face, which shone in the sun, red, bloated, covered in scars, and then I turned away, looked out at sea.

I know, he said. But if I were Christ, you'd be John, isn't that right? You'd be my beloved disciple, my

John. Because I know you love me more than the others. I love you more than them and you love me more, too. Isn't that right? It is, I know it is.

I don't remember what happened after that. I mean, I remember, but I don't want to talk about it. That's enough.

No, man, I don't want to. I don't feel like it.

Enough.

That's my right, isn't it?

I think about it a lot. About hatred, I mean, and fear. I think about it and wonder which comes first. Is hatred born out of fear, or is fear born of hatred? And I wonder what will happen to us, what tomorrow will bring, where all this is headed. I wonder what kind of country we'll be living in, us and those who come after us. A country that will exist because it hates and fears? A country that will exist in order to hate and fear? And I want to believe in something. I need something to believe in, you know? Something, someone to believe in. I need to believe in some new Christ, even if I know he doesn't exist, even if I know he'll never descend to earth, never be born, or crucified, or resurrected. To know that something doesn't exist and to believe in it anyhow – that, I think, is the only salvation left to us. Because if you believe in something that doesn't exist, maybe – who knows, maybe – one day the thing you believe in will appear.

—◦◦◦—

It must have been around five when they showed up. The Ikariot and Draou up front, the other three in the bed of the truck – we'd never seen them before, and we never saw them after that, either. We were surprised, to tell the truth – what were Xellinakis's goons doing up here on Easter – but we never imagined what was about to happen. You might ask, if we had, what would that have changed, what could we have done? I don't know. Things might have been different. Maybe if we'd guessed from the beginning what they had in mind, things might have unfolded differently. Maybe, I don't know.

They passed right by us and went and settled in under the shelter. Right off the bat the smoke started drifting our way. They were plastered, even worse than us. And the speakers in the truck were screeching full blast, fiddles and dari dari and all that island crap.

Dari dari dari dari, the gulls are fucking on the seashore, Tasos shouted.

He was ready for a fight, but Magda held him back. She pulled him aside, shook him by the arm. He didn't pay any mind.

That asshole, he kept saying. The coward, the bully, what a disgrace of a human. On a holiday like this he sends his punks to spoil our fun. He can't just leave us alone, fuck him and his whole family, fuck them all. The fucking disgrace.

We went over, too, to try and calm him down – fuck it, we said, they'll get bored, they'll leave.

To make a long story short, we set up shop under the trees and pretended nothing was going on. The women brought out the sweets and lit the camp stoves to make coffee. Then they came over to take the rest of our wine away, but we sent them packing.

Sitting there under the trees, someone said something about how much he hurts for this country. I don't remember who it was – we were all plastered, twelve sheets to the wind – but he said, I feel this country beating like a heart inside me. It's like having two hearts. And someone else said that he wanted to fall asleep, into a deep, heavy sleep and wake up years later, after all this was over. And someone else said maybe if something really bad were to happen, like a big earthquake, maybe they'd take pity on us and let us live. If there was a big earthquake and lots of people died, maybe they would finally say, look at those poor Greeks and the terrible thing that happened to them. They might take pity on us, might let us off the hook, let us live. That's the kind of stuff they were saying. The kind of talk you find at the bottom of a bottle. Women's talk. It's true. If you talk and talk and talk, sooner or later you end up talking like a woman. I turned to look at Tasos, but he was looking in the other direction, at the rats who had settled in under the shelter and were shouting and laughing as if they had the whole place to themselves.

Then someone – not someone, the kid from Larissa who works for Theodorakis with the blond girl – said, look over there. We looked and saw an upside-down triangle in the sky. The sun had gone behind the clouds and the light was making an upside-down triangle that rose up as far as the eye could see. And we all said we'd never seen anything like it before, it was the first time we'd seen the sunlight making an upside-down triangle in the sky, and someone said, it's a bad sign. But Tasos said, no, look again, look, it's not a triangle, it's a victory sign – we're going to win, he said, and made the victory sign, and then, I remember, Kostis came running over and wrapped his fingers around Tasos's and said, Dad, your fingers look like rabbit's ears, and he squeezed Tasos's fingers in his little fist as if he were holding a rabbit by the ears, and I remember – I remember everything – I remember Tasos's eyes, I remember how he smiled, lips together so his teeth wouldn't show, I remember how he looked at the kid's fingers gripping his, how the victory sign disappeared into the kid's fist, and now you're asking me to tell you about things that can't be said, things it isn't right to talk about – and I can't do that, it's like you're asking me to tell you what color hatred is, or the face of a person who feels hate gnawing at his guts like the rat in that Chinese torture, when they strap a metal basin to your belly, upside-down with a rat trapped inside, and then light coals on top of the basin and the whole thing heats up and the rat inside goes nuts and starts to gnaw at your flesh trying to find a way out. Hatred. Hate. A rat in your guts.

After that, when Kostis went back to play ball with

the other kids, Tasos jumped up and fired the pistol into the air, looking straight at the rats who were sitting under the shelter. And then that rotting carcass of an Ikariot stood up slowly and heavily and went over and opened the door of the truck and pulled out his rifle and fired into the air, too, and we heard buckshot falling like rice on the leaves of the trees above our heads. Magda ran over and grabbed Tasos and made him sit down. He did as she asked, but he wouldn't hand over the gun.

OK, he said to her. That was the last time. I'm telling you, it's fine.

—❧—

We stared out at the sea. I remember us staring silently at the sea, remember wondering in my drunken haze how such a crowd of people could stay so silent for so long. Then Tasos said his piece about good coming from the sea because the sea has no memory, water doesn't remember. And I remember him saying that we need to be like water, too, and blot out all the old stuff, forget the old stuff and make a new beginning. He said we have to forget that what united us for all those years was money – stolen or honest, it doesn't matter – and that what unites us now is the fact that we no longer have that money. We have to forget all that and find something new to bring us together, he said. I remember him saying that this was his greatest dream and his greatest anxiety – to find something other than money that could unite us. Because he was sure that evil's greatest victory was in convincing us, in managing to make us all believe that we came into the world to look after only ourselves. Evil triumphs when we all try to make something of ourselves, rather than do something important beyond ourselves. And trying to make something of ourselves, looking out only for ourselves, is the great gift we give, each day, all of us, to the people who want to control our fate. We want to be like them because they've convinced us that we're how they'd like us to be – weak, insignificant, inferior. They succeeded in making us see ourselves through their eyes, instead of through our own. They convinced us that their way is the only way.

I may be wrong, though, Tasos said. I don't know. Sometimes I lose my faith, too, I really do. There are moments when I wonder, when I think that in order for us to rebuild this country all over again from scratch, we first have to rebuild ourselves from scratch, too.

Moments when I think that in order for us to find something new to unite us, we first have to go our separate
ways. How did that one guy put it? Every so often we
have to lose our minds in order to come to our senses.
So I wonder if maybe we first have to stop being what we
are so that later we can become what we want to be. So
we can all get out of here, escape, all of us, and scatter
all over the world. To become what the Jews used to be,
to become the Jews of the twenty-first century, of the
new millennium. Didn't Christ say it, too? You first have
to lose your soul in order to save it. That's how it is with
us, too. In order for us to be saved, we first have to be
lost. In order to save Greece, to save our country, first
we have to lose it.

That's the sort of thing Tasos was saying, I remember,
and I remember his eyes were even redder than
before, and then he raised his hand and pointed up
toward the sky and said, I'll miss all this, though, I'll
miss it so much, and most of all I'll miss the light, where
will we ever find light like this again, other places don't
have light like this – and then someone jumped up, it
might have been Psis, or Tremo, and shouted, what is all
this shit, man, what's all this bullshit you've been selling

us about Jews and millennia, what are you, some kind of mason or something? – and then a huge argument broke out, because others jumped in and said it's all the Jews' fault, they're the ones who destroyed Greece, and someone said that the whole mess is all a Jewish plot, for two thousand years they've feared and hated the Greeks, and since in all that time they couldn't destroy us any other way, they finally fixed it so that we'd all be in debt to the banks, which they control, because that's the only way they could tie us hand and foot and make us their slaves, and someone else said he read on the internet that the only people the Jews are afraid of are the Greeks, since back in the time of Alexander the Great we managed to enslave them not with battles and armies but with our language and culture and philosophy, and those motherfuckers never forgave us for it, those goatherds, those animal thieves. Someone else said that Christ was an agent for the masons, too, and they only backed him because they wanted to destroy ancient Greece, which is exactly what happened in the end. Another guy said it's the Jews who won't let us dig for oil all these years, too, we could've been one of the richest countries in the world, and another guy said it's not just oil, we've got tons of gold and uranium, his wife's cousin is in the port police, one of those gull cops, and he said some cagey types started poking around outside Kamenes the other day, and these frogmen combat diver guys went down to the sea floor with special machines and found out it's covered in gold from the volcano – they said they were scientists, researching the earthquakes, but who believes that, they're probably agents too. Someone else said that's why they've been trying so hard to destroy us these past few years, those faggot foreigners and our fucking traitor politicians, because Greece has oil and gold and uranium and osmium, which goes for thirteen million dollars a kilo on the open market, and red mercury which sells at twelve million, and they're using it all to build nuclear weapons and fuel for warheads and space ships, and if you look on the internet you'll see that there are these ancient books from India where it says the Greeks were the first humans to build space ships and they used red mercury for fuel, and of course the masons and their agents know all that, which is why all these years they've kept us under their thumb, fighting among ourselves, because if they let us free, Greece would be a superpower for sure and we'd have them all sucking our balls, Jews, Germans, Americans, everyone – and then two or three of the newcomers jumped in, Manos who works at the greenhouses and a few others, they turned to Stathis who works security at the asylum down in Rigos and said, Stathis, man, why don't you go down and bring up your net and paddy-wagon to nab these guys, this whole crew is dying for straitjackets, seriously, if jerking off could fuel space ships, Greeks would have gotten to the edge of the universe, maybe beyond. Then a huge argument broke out and everyone started fighting with everyone else, and I turned, I remember, and asked Tasos if he really believed that good would come from the sea – I remember saying, I don't care what it even means, I don't know what kind of good it'll be or how it'll come from the sea, just tell me if you really believe it, tell me if I should believe it, too, if it's worth my waiting for, if there's still hope, if there's any sense in waiting. And I remember that Tasos said, sure, of course it's worth waiting for good to come from the sea, because only when you finally realize that there's no sense in waiting for good to come does it actually start to make sense to wait – and that's true of everything in life, he said, because life only starts to mean something once you understand that life has no meaning, and then, I remember, I turned and looked at him because it seemed so strange for Tasos to be saying something like that – it seemed like a strange thing to be coming from a grocer, a guy who worked in the fields, who sold cucumbers and tomatoes at the farmer's market. And I suddenly felt ashamed because I realized he was ashamed that I was looking at him like that, and then he raised his glass and laughed – it's just the wine, he said, when I drink I talk pretty big, all kinds of fairytale shit.

I know, I said. It's fine, I'm the same way.

Now that you mention it, I said, all of life is a fairytale, a story you tell yourself. That's what life is. A fairytale you create in your head. A story about the place where you live and the places you used to live. The things you experience every day. The people around you – men, women, children, relatives, friends, neighbors, colleagues, enemies, strangers. The things that happen and those that should happen and those you wish would happen. And then something happens and the story ends and you have to make another story, if you want to keep on living. You have to create another story in this new place where they sent you to live, in a new place with new people. If you want to survive, you struggle to make that story. You struggle to fit new places and people into this new fairytale you're creating. You have to fight that fight, to struggle for that story. To build a new world, with caves and streams, plane trees, chapels nestled on hills, stony cliffs and sandy vineyards, rowboats, anchors, oars. And in order to create that new world, you first have to create a new self. New eyes, new ears, a new tongue, nose, hands. Because that's the only way for you to learn new images, new sounds, new smells and tastes. You have to learn the sea and the weather and how the winds blow in winter and summer. You have to learn not to be scared when the sirocco uproots trees and sends stones tumbling, not to be scared by the smell of wild arum or when you hear shearwaters crying in the dark or the wooden stairs creaking on August nights. You have to learn how to unhook a bluefish without it cutting your fingers and how to kill a moray eel by pouring vinegar on its head. And then, when you've finally managed to build your new world, you'll be gripped by the fear that something will happen and this world, too, will end, and you'll have to go in search of another, and another, and another. But for how long? How many worlds can fit into one world? How many lives in one life? How many lives does one person need in order to keep living?

And then I saw Lena leaning over me, shaking me by the shoulders.

You're babbling. Do you hear me? You're babbling again. Pull yourself together, you're making fools of us. Fuck it, don't you even care for the kid's sake? I mean, you could give a shit about me. But the kid?

———❦———

I wish the day hadn't ended the way it did. I really do. But each of us has a story to live, and it has to end how it has to end, like it or not.

So the kids were playing ball and at some point they kicked it over by the shelter and Kostis ran to get it. And that stinking carcass from Ikaria held it there with his foot and wouldn't give it back. He said something to the kid and laughed and the others laughed, too. And Kostis stood there with his hands together behind his back, twisting his fingers together, head bent as if he

– 72 –

were listening to some voice rising from the ground. Magda ran over and grabbed him by the arm and the guy from Ikaria took his foot off the ball and kicked it as far as he could. Magda said something and the guy said something back and all the rats laughed. We weren't close enough to hear, we never found out what he said, but when Magda turned back around she had two red stains on her cheeks and her mouth was trembling as if she'd kissed a snake.

That's when Tasos jumped to his feet and ran to the shelter and stood in front of the rats and pointed the gun at the Ikariot's head. I remember it perfectly, I remember as if it were happening now, I remember it all, the things that happened and the things that didn't and the things that should have happened. And then the Ikariot stood up slowly from his bench and raised both hands to straighten the bandana he was wearing on his head and walked right past Tasos, who kept the gun trained on him, following his steps with the gun, and opened the door of the truck and pulled out the rifle, loaded it and went and stood in front of Tasos with the rifle in one hand as if it were toy gun from Carnival, aiming straight at Tasos's head.

Each of them was aiming at the other's head.

How much time passed?

Each of them was aiming at the other's head.

We held Magda back so she wouldn't go running over. We men held Magda back, and the women gathered the children to one side as they started to cry. Our hearts flopped in our chests like a fish being unhooked and tossed back into the sea. We men thought Tasos would be the first to pull the trigger. It's true. I said I would tell you everything. We were waiting for that, and wanted it. We wanted to see Tasos pull the trigger, wanted to see the Ikariot's head explode, burst like a watermelon. Then we would all rush over, all of us, men, women, and children, and we would crush him, tear his body into a thousand pieces. That's what we wanted, that's what our hearts longed to see. One rat fewer in the world. One fat rat fewer.

We didn't care about what would happen after that.

Each of them was aiming at the other's head.

How much time must have passed?

Each of them was aiming at the other's head.

And then Tasos lowered his arm.

Put that thing in your pocket, or I'll shove it up your ass, the Ikariot said.

His voice was calm, indifferent, almost bored.

And Tasos obeyed and put the gun in his back pocket and then the Ikariot lowered the rifle and went over and slapped him on the face. Not a punch, a slap. As if Tasos was one of the whores from his titty bar. And the slap wasn't full of hatred or anger, more like pity, as if he were doing him a favor, as if it was for his own good.

Now get out of here, fool, he said. Pick up your dick and go.

And for a moment our hearts flopped in our chests again, because we thought that Tasos would surely pull the gun back out and this time he would pull the trigger. But he didn't, he didn't do anything, he didn't even say a word. He just turned and headed in our direction with his head down, then turned back around again and went and stood at the mouth of the cave. He stood there at the mouth of the cave – a little drop of a man before all that black. He stood and looked at us, his eyes as red as can be, and his face red too, his scars seemed to have swollen and his whole face looked like a mask that someone held up to the fire until it slowly started to melt. He pulled the gun from his pocket and said something that none of us heard, then disappeared into the cave at a run.

Then the Ikariot turned around, looked at us, stomped his foot on the ground as if trying to chase off a bunch of mutts, and shouted, back up, you foreign bitches! It didn't make much sense, because none of us had even moved.

Back up, he shouted. I'll swallow your dreams. Get the fuck back.

He whistled to the others, and they all got into the truck and left.

Then Magda broke away and ran howling toward the cave, but we caught her before she went in, too. She was hitting herself, crying, shouting his name. The other women formed a circle around her, trying to calm her down – don't be like that, he's a man, he's drunk and ashamed, his pride is wounded, he'll get over it. Calm down, remember the kids, don't go doing anything crazy. As soon as he sobers up, he'll come out and everything will be fine. Calm down, listen, think of the kids. It was just a bad moment, it'll pass.

Time passed, night fell, and most of our crowd left

with their wives and children. Two or three of us stayed behind with Magda to wait. Every so often we'd venture into the cave with our flashlights, calling out Tasos's name, but nothing. By then Magda was exhausted, had shrunk into a corner and was talking to herself. Good will come from the sea, she kept saying over and over, like a song. Or a dirge, who knows. We lit a fire but no one felt any warmer – the air was freezing, and the drink had worn off, and we were shivering. And we couldn't even talk. What was there to say? We tried to say something to console her, but she didn't want to hear any of it – she had already written him off.

His eyes, she said. That's how I knew. For a long time now his eyes have been the color of death.

Have you ever sat around a fire at night with a bunch of silent people? It drives you wild. I mean it. You watch the flickering flames and the shadows transforming the others' faces into strange masks, and you listen to the sizzling fire and the crackling wood and the wind whistling through the branches of the trees – and soon enough, you start to see and hear other things, things coming alive in the dark that surrounds you, and you feel afraid, a fear that seems to come from a long time ago, from back when people still lived in caves, and it creeps up your back, grabs hold of you, grips you by the shoulders. And then you begin to wonder whether the fire is what brought those things to life in the night, if perhaps it would be better to put the fire out and become one with the dark, to try and fool those things in the dark, to make them believe we're not any different, we're just like them, we too are things of the dark, and suddenly you find yourself caught between two fears, between a fear born from fire and a fear born from darkness, and you don't know what to do, you don't know which of the two fears is worse, which of those two fears to choose.

And then another fear grips you, a bigger one, because you realize how terrifying it is, how terrifying that you've begun to react not like a person but like something else, that no person would ever wonder whether light is worse than darkness, whether the fear born of fire is worse than the fear born of darkness. And what scares you most of all is that you don't know what that other thing is that you've started to become – what will come next, what does a person become when he stops being a person, what is there on the other side of human?

Then you think how, in the end, this is what that poor bastard Tasos was trying to do. He may not have known it, but he was struggling to stay human, to keep on being a person. Not a good person, or a proper person, or a better person, just a person – a person, plain and simple. And he sought to help us keep being people, too, so we wouldn't become that other thing that wonders whether light is worse than darkness. He disappeared not because of Xellinakis or that asshole Ikariot, or tomatoes or onions or imazalil or thiabenda-zole or Senegalese sea bream or the suites at Niktaris's hotel or even justice or solidarity, but because of the light. The light. Because he wanted to stop us before we became that other thing that wonders whether light is worse than darkness.

Fairy tales, you'll say, big talk, drunk talk, and you're probably right. Calm down, you'll say. Give it a rest, because before you know it you'll be telling us that Tasos the vegetable guy, who sold cucumbers and tomatoes at the farmer's market, was some kind of philosopher and revolutionary to boot. Light and darkness, what a load of bull. What do you people know about this kind of thing, anyhow? You're farmers, security guys, plastic guys from the warehouses, Salamanders, Tomises, Charonises, what do you know about all that? You're foreigners here, you should stick to speaking foreignish, thinking all your outsider thoughts. Food, work, sleep – and maybe a fresh young thing right off the boat every now and then so you can blow off some steam. That's all you're good for. Anything above that is for the people above. That's what you'll tell me, and you'd be right. But then again, you don't know what it's like to live here. If you knew, if you lived on this island, too, if you were an outsider, you might see things differently. We here are like blind people who weren't born blind. Like people who can't see the sun anymore, but know it exists, remember what it's like, and bit by bit start to hate the sun for still existing when they can't see it anymore, and then they start to hate the people who can still see the sun, too. And Tasos was the guy struggling to make us blind folk not hate the sun and not hate the people who can still see it. So even though none of us believed the stuff he said, we still wanted to hear him say it. We wanted to know there was someone among us who believed we're better than what we've become. That everything isn't dead inside of us, that we still carry things inside that we can love, even if we don't know what they are or what they'll become, the way a mother loves her child even before it's born.

If you lived here, too, if you were a foreigner, an outsider, you might see things differently. Maybe, I don't know.

The next morning a whole crowd went up to the Refuge, cops, firemen, volunteers with helmets and ropes. They went about three hundred meters into the cave, until they came to a precipice and stopped because it would have been dangerous, even deadly, for them to go any further. They went back in the next day and the day after that, and shouted and searched all around with their flashlights, and turned up a big fat nothing. In the end they decided that Tasos must have fallen off the ledge, so they gathered up their equipment and left – though no one could explain how he managed to get so deep into the cave when he was walking in the dark with no light, no nothing.

There was no funeral, of course. Just before school let out for the summer, Magda took the kids and went back to Athens. Meanwhile the whole island heard about what happened with the Ikariot, but no one did anything about it – who would dare speak up? I mean, not even Tasos's wife said a thing, so why would strangers get involved? A month or so later Elvis disappeared, and then Lazaros's son, and everyone said bad things come in threes, so now we were done, and bit by bit the whole thing was forgotten.

There's nothing else to tell you, we're through. The end. If you want details, go and ask one of those people who likes talking about blood and brains on the ground and that kind of thing. About tears and dirges and dreams of dead men. But even they would tell you the same thing. How we were all dying for Tasos to pull the trigger that afternoon, to blow the Ikariot's brains into the air, rather than his own. How we all expected him to give us a proper ending, heroic, manly. And it makes no difference how it actually happened. It doesn't matter if he blew out his own brains or fell into the hole or got eaten by werewolves in the cave or who knows what else. No difference at all. None, none at all. Betrayal is betrayal.

A major betrayal.

And since then we've been waiting.

We still go up to the Refuge every so often and do

our thing, just like before. But these days, when night falls, we sit around the fire and look out at the sea as if expecting something, as if waiting for something to happen. And if sometimes someone jumps up in his drunkenness and starts in on some lament, about how and why – why a man like that had to meet such an unjust end, and why we let him run into the cave and why no one ran in after him, why not one of us went in to drag him back out, and how afraid he must have been walking in the darkness all alone, and how he must have waited, whether he got scared at some point and tried to find the way back out, how he must have waited for us to come in and save him, how he must have cried and called our names until he finally lost hope, and why we did it, how could we have done such a thing, what kind of people were we, what kind of people had we become, how had our hearts gotten so hard – and if one of us starts, in his drunkenness, to talk like that we all jump on him and tell him to shut it. We don't want to talk about the past, we don't want to look back, only forward. We don't want to look toward the cave but out to sea, at the open waters. Without talking too much, without tears and laments, without memories.

We sit there silently around the fire and look out at the sea, as if we're expecting some true hero to come from there one day, some hero who's not a war hero but a hero for what comes after a war, a hero who's alive, not dead, a hero who'll throb not with death but with life, a hero not for the dead but for those who continue to live.

When you look down at it from above, our island resembles a pair of handcuffs. Uneven handcuffs – one bigger than the other, as if made for someone with one atrophied arm. Little Handcuff and Big Handcuff, Outer Island and Inner Island, Upper Part and Lower Part. Our island is two islands, two handcuffs, and the chain linking the two, which we call the Doors, is a long, narrow strip of land, twelve kilometers from end to end. Each of the two islands has a lake in the middle – Apsithia, or Wormwood, on Big Handcuff, and Little Handcuff has Second Coming. Above Apsithia rises the highest mountain, Polemos, Mount War, from whose peak you can see eleven islands: Ios, Sikinos, Santorini, Milos, Kimolos, Polivos, Sifnos, Syros, Paros, Antiparos, and Naxos. On good days, when the wind blows the hoar-frost from the horizon, you can see even further, to Amorgos and Astipalia, and to the south, eighty miles away, the snows of the Psiloreitis mountain.

My father says that a day will come, soon, when our island will split right down the middle, where the Doors *are now, and become two islands. He's always saying things like that, ever since he had his stroke. It's a matter of time, he says. Can it really just be chance that we've been having so many earthquakes recently? Or that the sea has started to warm again over in Kamenes? All that happened back in 1956, too, and then the earthquake came and not a stone was left standing. He says half the town collapsed back then, and the sea rose three hundred meters above the shoreline and Meskinia was cut off from the main island and became a rocky little islet. These are signs, he says. Just like back then, it's the same way now, too. Only now it'll be worse. Now the end is coming. The real, final end.*

My father. He was always a bit of a character, but since the stroke he's gone off the rails entirely. He's only fifty, but he talks like an old woman on death's door who sees cherubim and visions in the sky. I sit there and feed him a few spoonfuls of soup, as much as he'll eat, and when he starts in on these things it makes the hairs on the back of my neck stand straight up. Earthquakes, volcanoes, tsunamis. I can't object, either, because the least little thing sets him off, he'll pull the blanket over his head and I have to plead with him for hours to come back out. And then he starts in on the other kind of crazy talk, like the other day after I'd fed him, when he started getting after me to chase the geese out of the room.

Get those geese out of here, he said. Just shoo the filthy things out, don't you pity your father at all? What are you, a daughter or a tyrant?

What could I do, I started waving my arms around in the air as if I were chasing geese away. He hadn't pulled that trick before, and it caught me off guard — it took me a while to figure out he was talking about the flies buzzing around his soup bowl.

They're all signs, my father says. The geese, the earthquakes, the sea temperature rising over by the volcano. And that's not all. When you see people disappearing into caves and fish coming out onto dry land and paralytics getting up out of their wheelchairs — when you see that sort of thing, you know the end is coming. The real end, the ultimate end, the good end.

That's the sort of thing he says, all day, every day. And at night, when he's tired, he takes my hand and rests it against his cheek, beside his lips, which are crooked and swollen and look like a little omicron that split down the middle and became an omega.

Don't leave, he says, his eyes closed. Stay here all night.

Stay here, so I can feel your sweat.

Kill the German

The procession is on its way, the bier of Christ. There go the bells. The procession will be passing by soon, and the old man is still locked in the room with the girl. Chronis pushes his wheelchair over to the window, hoping for some clue as to what's going on. Nothing. Lights off, curtains drawn. Though today he brought her upstairs earlier than usual. Around six, maybe even five-thirty. So something's up.

He busts a move with the chair – reverse, half turn to the right, half turn to the left, straight ahead, again to the right – then wheels himself back to the desk. The scorpion has scrambled up onto the tallest rock, in the middle of the tank, and is sitting there utterly still, waiting. Chronis breaks off a lump of bread and dips it in the wine, then works it between his fingers until he's shaped a tiny little pie, as thin and round as a coin. He lifts the thick, flat stone off the lid of the tank, which is long and narrow, like a miniature ballot box, and drops the coin of bread through the slit in the top. These past few days the scorpion hasn't been at its best. It only comes out for water, seems to have no appetite at all. It didn't even touch the spiders, its favorite treat. Chronis was alarmed, though of course he knows the scorpion can survive without eating for weeks, even months. He experimented with various things, even tried throwing night moths into the tank, not to mention an entire lizard, which he spat blood to catch with a net over by the ruins of Drakomanolis's place. Then yesterday or the day before, out of curiosity, he tossed in a crumb of bread soaked in wine, and soon enough the scorpion crept out from under the broken roof tile and slowly approached the bread. It circled it once, swiped at it a couple of times, then suddenly leapt forward and grabbed the little coin with its pincers and started manically stabbing the bread with its tail, spinning in a circle all the while, stabbing it over and over, as if the bread were a living creature resisting its poison. Then, when the bread was nothing more than crumbs, the scorpion went over to the side of the tank and started to tap on the glass with its tail, as if asking for more. Tap tap tap. Tap tap tap. Tap tap tap.

Chronis replaces the stone over the slit and pushes his wheelchair back to get a better view. He makes his hands into fists, stacks one on the other, and rests his chin on the top.

He waits.

The scorpion doesn't move.

Why do you have a scorpion? asked the guy who came to fix the internet.

It helps me remember, said Chronis.

The guy made a *pss pss* sound as if he were calling a cat, tapped the glass with his finger, bent down over the tank.

Does it have a name?

Kermit. Sometimes I call him Gregor Samsa. Depending on my mood.

The guy looked sideways at Chronis and then back at the scorpion.

Kermit, huh?

Yep, said Chronis. And I call the canary Sylvester, and the snake Eve.

———

Chronis stares at the scorpion and feels it staring back at him with its twelve eyes. He wonders what it would be like to see the world through twelve eyes. He looks at the scorpion's tawny body, its eight legs which have blended in with the rock, and its tail sticking up in a perfect curve, the stinger hanging from the end like a bitter black tear.

He waits.

The scorpion doesn't move.

Dtan dtan dtan. The churchbells ring heavily, as if in revenge, like a hammer intent not on nailing, but on punishing the nail.

Dtan dtan dtan.

The procession will be coming soon, and the old man is still locked in the room with the girl. It happens every evening. And each night when the girl emerges and slowly descends the stairs, gripping the rusted handrail, she seems thinner and weaker, her skin more sallow, her hair less blond, as if her face is absorbing the yellow from her hair. Day by day, night by night, she descends the stairs more slowly, her head bent lower and her knees weaker, as if some terrible creature is hidden in that room, a dragon sucking the girl's blood, sucking her strength, day by day, night by night. Chronis knows he has to do something, there has to be something he can do to keep the girl from climbing those stairs, to keep the old geezer from locking her in the room, and though he knows what he needs to do, he isn't sure he should, because virtue isn't an ideology or a religion, nor is love – if they were, people on the Christian right and the Christian left would be the best, most benevolent people in the world, and you can see for yourself how most of them are, crooked rascals whose eyes shine with hypocrisy, woe to they who feel love and kindness out of ideological commitment, woe to they who turn Christ into a religion, which is to say an ideology – and since the entire anti-authoritarian ethic rests on the denial of authority, that denial can't itself be denied, even in the name of virtue or love, because then we'd have to admit that the ethic is subject to the tyranny of relativity, in which case the anti-authoritarian individual becomes not an opponent of tyranny but a slave to two tyrannies – first, of authority, and second, of relativity – and consequently whatever action Chronis takes, while by no means guaranteed to bring about a positive result, will most certainly result in several evils. Besides the fact that, if we really want to tell it like it is, intervening in others' lives is also a demonstration of power, of authority. And don't try and tell me it matters whether the goal of that intervention is good or bad. Don't you dare try to unload that one on me, because it's the worst Manichaeism of all: good power, bad power. Am I right or am I right?

Something like that, at any rate.

Then again, if you refuse to accept either relativism (nothing is entirely white or black) or Manichaeism (everything is either white or black), maybe there's something else going on? Maybe you need to get yourself checked? Maybe you've lost your bearings? Maybe you can't even be sure that two and two make four?

The guy who came to fix the internet plugged everything back in, then stood up and started to gather his tools. He threw another sideways glance at Chronis's legs.

Car accident?

Vibrator.

Vibrator?

I set a bomb in a sex shop, slipped on my way out, and crushed both legs.

Chronis waits.

He waits, his gaze fixed on the scorpion, as if he too were a scorpion with eight, ten, twelve eyes.

He waits.

Then, with an astonishing move, the scorpion leaps like a tawny shadow from the top of the rock and lands on the coin of bread, lifts half its body into the air, grips the coin between its pincers, and stabs the bread with its black stinger.

Chronis raises his head and exhales and feels half his body unclenching, relaxing – it's been a long time since he felt the other half, from the waist down. Though sometimes he does. He feels it like a mass of pain, a monumental, ghostly pain, a pain both seen and unseen, a pain more terrible than any other, the pain of flesh that isn't flesh, of legs that aren't legs, pain the size of god, a godly pain, which exists yet remains invisible, a pain that hurts like two pains, because it's born of a body – or half a body, anyhow – both visible and nonexistent.

Chronis raises his head and looks out the window. Across the street the door to the room is still shut, lights off, curtains drawn.

Dtan dtan dtan. The sound of the bells hammers into his temples.

Dtan dtan dtan.

He looks back at the tank and sees that the scorpion has already started to knead the bread, the soft insides of bread baptized in wine – what a rare scorpion, the only of its kind, *Androctonus artophagus*. Or perhaps *Androctonus artocrasophagus* would be more appropriate?

Take, eat; this is my body, says Chronis.

Drink of it, all of you, he says. This is my blood.

Amen.

—◆—

Between the tolling of the churchbells he can hear his mother's snoring. A maestro in the chair yet his cock won't crow.

He spins the wheelchair around and goes back to the window. It's May. Which means something. It means something that Easter fell in May this year. He read about it the other day on the internet, but already forgot – which is a good thing. On the one hand he's annoyed that he forgot so quickly what it means that Easter fell in May, he doesn't want to forget anything, he'd prefer to remember everything, because memory is truth, memory is love, memory is life, but on the other hand he's glad he forgot, because it gives him another challenge: to remember what it means that Easter fell in May without using the internet. The internet destroys your memory because there's no need to remember anything anymore – you just push a button and it's all there before you. But if you abolish memory you abolish everything, you abolish truth, love, life. And if you abolish this life here, if you squander your life in this world, you squander your eternal life, too, because memory on its own is handicapped, memory on its own is a paralyzed, crippled body. It's not enough just to remember. The memory of fire doesn't warm the body any more than the memory of water refreshes it. If you want to get warm, it isn't enough to remember a fire's warmth – you have to actually light one. If you want to quench a thirst it isn't enough to remember water – you have to drink it. Life requires action. And if you squander your life here you squander your eternal life, too, because only those who live their lives on earth to the fullest will also live eternally, since the only path from this life to eternal life is life itself, not death – death is nothing.

Or something like that.

But back to the old man. He's late. He's taking a long time tonight. Which means something. It must mean something. And yet Chronis knows that no matter how much he searches on the internet he won't find out what. No matter how much he searches, he won't find out why the old geezer has been locked in the room with the girl for so many hours tonight. And they say technology is king. Find out in seconds flat how many times a person blinks every day, how many wads of chewed gum you'll find per square meter on the sidewalks of Caracas, how many days of sunshine there are in Mongolia every year, how many women in Europe conceive a child in a bed bought at IKEA, how many families in America sign their dog's or cat's name on their Christmas cards. But you won't ever find out why the old man has been locked in the room with the girl for so many hours. The internet will never tell you that. Never.

Between the tolling of the churchbells he can hear his mother's snoring. A maestro in the chair yet his cock won't crow.

A nice Lenten cocktail was just what the doctor ordered for his mother.

Recipe for Lenten Cocktail Caipillinha Number 2
    Ingredients:
    1 shot Xanax (1 mg)
    1 shot Seroxat (30 mg)
    1 shot Cymbalta (30 mg)
    1 shot Remeron (45 mg)
    1 glass water (preferably bottled)
    Preparation:
    Put all the ingredients in your palm at once (except
    for the water).
    Close your fist and shake well.
    Use the water to swallow the mixture.
    (Note: if preferred, drink the water through a straw.)
    Maybe I should've been a bartender, Chronis says.

This place is to blame. No doubt. The island is to blame
for sure. On an island there's nowhere to hide. In a city
you're a stranger among strangers but don't feel like
one because everyone is. Here, on the island, everyone
knows you, you know everyone, and yet you feel like
a stranger because that's what you'll always be. Islands
are contrary to human nature. The sea is contrary to

human nature. Only monsters can survive on islands. Monsters or gods. Look at Christ. Only he could walk on the waves. Only he who conquers death can conquer the sea. The sea is hell. Hell is the sea surrounding an island. That's what hell is. A speck of land with sea all around. Without a doubt. Look at Christ. Learn to see. Look at Christ.

Good evening, friends. Tonight we have a guest in our studio, Chronis Petrakis. Chronis – do you mind if I call you Chronis, Chronis? (laughter) – is an individual with mobility issues. He's also what we call an internal migrant. Two years ago he left Piraeus and settled on an island in the Aegean, his ancestral island. Chronis, good evening and welcome (applause).

Good evening, Nikos. Thank you for having me.

So, Chronis, tell us. How difficult was your move from the city to the island?

Well, Nikos, it certainly wasn't easy. No one's yet invented a floating wheelchair, and journeys by boat are always uncomfortable. But thanks to the Virgin Mary and Saint Nicholas, we managed. All's well that ends well.

As Shakespeare would say.

As Shakespeare would say, that's precisely right. And now that we're here, life on the island turns out to be pretty exciting. After all, as John Donne would say, no man is an island – and if the sea washes away even a clod of the soil here, Europe is that much smaller.

Exquisite words. What you just said about Europe getting smaller, Chronis, could really serve as a reminder to our European partners and friends – and we may need some scare quotes there, ladies and gentlemen – who've been hatching their own plans for the proud, long-suffering citizens of this nation. Exquisite, insightful words. Can you repeat that bit, Chronis? We'd all like to hear.

If the sea washes away even a clod of our soil, Europe is that much smaller.

There it is, friends (applause). That's great, Chronis, thanks so much. And I have to say, I'm a huge fan of *Miami Vice*, but I didn't remember John Donne ever talking about islands and Europe and so on. You caught me unawares.

It's OK, Nikos. It's not so terrible to be caught unawares every now and then. The real problem is when they catch you in your underwear.

Ha, unawares, underwear. Excellent, very clever (laughter). That's a good one, friends (applause).

Thanks, Nikos. I guess it wasn't too bad. Do you know the other one, about Don Johnson?

Hahahaha. Chronis Petrakis, ladies and gents. A real one-of-a-kind guy. Let's take a short commercial break, we'll be back in a minute.

Here we are back in the studio with tonight's guest, Chronis Petrakis. So, Chronis.

So, Nikos.

We were talking about your new life on the island. Tell us about your experiences during these many months. Can you describe your daily routine?

Well, Nikos, I can tell that you and your faithful audience nourish a deep love for the art of poetry, so permit me to answer not in my own words but with a few lines by Anne Sexton.

Anne Sexton, of course. What a singer she is, what a voice (applause).

Sure, Nikos. Poet, singer, Shakespeare, Sexton, sex addict, it's all more or less the same. And I have to say, I've found tonight's show quite sexy. It's been sexcellent.

There it is again, folks (laughter). Chronis Petrakis,

ladies and gents (applause). A true original, that's for sure. Well, we're all ears.

> *I am rowing, I am rowing*
> *though the wind pushes me back*
> *and I know that that island will not be perfect*
> *it will have the flaws of life,*
> *the absurdities of the dinner table,*
> *but there will be a door*
> *and I will open it*
> *and I will get rid of the rat inside me,*
> *the gnawing pestilential rat.*
> *God will take it with his two hands*
> *and embrace it.*

Tap tap tap.

Chronis goes back to the window and looks across the way. Lights out, curtains drawn. He knows what he needs to do, but he doesn't know if he should. And if he does, he needs to hurry, because the procession will be passing by any minute. Just listen to the bells. The procession will be here any minute. How tragic it all is. A quadruple tragedy. A quadriplegic tragedy. Let's review our notes. Tragedy number one: the most suitable way to save the girl is for someone to report the old man to the competent state authorities (a tragedy that in fact comprises two sub-tragedies, or perhaps tragedettes, in keeping with the tragically diminutive aspect of that to which we refer – namely, tragedette number one: competent; and tragedette number two: state authorities). Tragedy number two: the only person who could report the old geezer is Chronis, but Chronis doesn't believe in reporting, or in state authorities, for that matter. Tragedy number three: the only other way to save the girl is for Chronis to take matters into his own hands, but Chronis is a cripple. Tragedy number four: even were Chronis to overcome this technical difficulty, he'd find himself face-to-face with another, more critical issue: if it's a crime for the old man to impose his will on the girl, why isn't it a crime for Chronis to impose his will on the old man, in order to make him stop imposing his will on the girl? Careful, now. Don't tell me that the ends justify the means, because I might just lose my cool. That's the kind of bullshit sophistry that got us where we are today.

Tap tap tap.

Chronis opens the window just a crack and listens, then closes it again. On the old man's roof across the way, a cat is sitting and staring at him with bright yellow eyes, as if it just ate a whole flock of canaries.

Tap tap tap.

Careful, I'm telling you, this is serious business. It's a major dilemma. The whole town knows that the old man locks the girl in the room each night. And the whole town knows why the old man locks the girl in the room each night. The whole town knows that the girl's mother knows why the old man locks the girl in the room each night. The whole town knows that the girl's mother knows what goes on in the room where the old man locks the girl each night. The whole town knows why the girl's mother lets the old man lock the girl in the room each night. Everyone knows everything, but no one does anything. Say that again. Everyone knows everything, but no one does anything. Say it again. Say it again, say it a thousand times like a riddle, an incantation, a little song.

Everyone knows everything, and everyone does nothing.

Everyone, everything, nothing.

Everyone, everything, nothing.

Everyone, everything, nothing.

Tap tap tap.

Everyone knows everything, and everyone does nothing.

And listen, the dilemma is really big. It's not ethical, or sociopoliticocultural. It's not a financial dilemma, either, though they say if the girl's mother didn't owe money to everyone with two nostrils, she wouldn't be handing her daughter over to that coffin-dodger every night. It's not even an existential dilemma. No, it's ontological. If everyone knows everything and does nothing, what does that make you, who also know everything and do nothing? You're just like them, you're the same as them, one of them. But if you do something, you'll stop being like them, stop being the same as them, one of them. If you act, if you find a way to bring an end to this mess, you'll be different. So choose: either you're like them or you're not. It's clear as day, the dilemma is ontological. Are you really who you are, or perhaps you just think you're who you are, whereas you're actually someone else, someone like them? Watch what you say. Watch what you don't say, too. Because unspoken words aren't words, and unperformed actions aren't actions. So watch it, be careful. You're responsible not only for what you say and do, but also for what you don't say and don't do.

Momentous words, sayings of great men, distillations of wisdom.

Tap tap tap.

Who's there?

At our window stands a bird
Tapping the glass with pleading words

Chronis looks out the window, doesn't see any birds and is glad.

Tap tap tap.

The scorpion is glued to the side of the tank, drumming the glass with its pincers.

Tap tap tap.

Chronis maneuvers his wheelchair – or, rather, his mobility device – his mo*biii*lity dev*iiice*, stress on the biii-ing and the ice, goes back to the desk, makes yet another coin of bread, and throws it into the tank.

The scorpion waits.

Chronis waits.

The girl's waiting, too, he hears a voice meow.

You shut your mouth, and keep your nose out of other people's business, Chronis says. Why don't you go catch a mouse or two, all those canaries are giving you jaundice.

—∞—

The world is constructed in such a way as to deprive each of us of the possibility of doing any personal good. No, that's not right. Let's take it from the top. Ready? OK. The world is constructed in such a way as to relieve each of us of the responsibility of doing any personal good. We're all free to do bad in a thousand ways, but good is always someone else's affair. In our societies, the state has a monopoly on good. In order for a society to function in even the most basic way, the state has to have a monopoly on violence – but even more crucial is for the state to have a monopoly on good. Does that seem like too much? A bit of an exaggeration? Yet it's the truth. No, that's not right. Yet that's how truth works. Just as power is synonymous with its own corruption – because power doesn't in fact corrupt, nor can it be corrupted, as any random fool on TV or the internet might say, but rather, power is synonymous with its own corruption, which is to say power equals corruption – and in the same way, truth is synonymous with its own transgression. Which means that in order to see the whole truth, you need to transgress it. In order to see truth in its entirety you have to get some distance, just as in order to see all of Earth, you have to travel thousands of kilometers into space.

Sir, sir.

Yes?

Well, sir, as Nietzsche said, I profit from a philosopher only to the extent that he can provide an example. So, can you give us an example?

Young man, I'm afraid I'm no philosopher. And Nietzsche was fit to be tied.

Fine, whatever. Just give us an example.

What kind of example?

Of what you were just saying. Good and the state and stuff.

And stuff.

What you were saying. Give us an example so we'll understand better.

OK. It's simple. Take the girl. The old geezer locks her in the room every night. What am I supposed to do about that? What's the good I'm supposed to do? I should tell the cops. Or the girl's teacher at school. Or Babajim, or some other priest. In each of those cases I'd be transferring onto individuals in positions of authority my own responsibility to enact good. That would be the ultimate moral failure. The other solution would be for me to take the situation into my own hands. To impose good directly. Yet imposition is itself tantamount to power. If I use violence to force the old man – and how else could I force him – to stop locking the girl in the room, I would be imposing my will, my power, on another person. Violence is the most extreme form of power, and murder is the most extreme form of violence. Therefore the destruction of life is the most extreme form of power. Inasmuch as –

Sir, sir, I have a question. Who's that Babajim you mentioned?

Come on, haven't you been paying any attention at all? Have I been talking to the air this whole time? He's the local priest, at the church of Saint Marina.

Why do you call him Babajim?

Because his name is Dimitris, and he can down a barrel of ouzo in a single sitting. Papa-Dimitris, Papa-Jim, Babajim.

Oh, after Babajim ouzo, huh? Fuck, that's a good one. You may not look it, but you're a pretty chill guy, sir. OK, we're listening.

As I was saying, murder is the most violent form of power. But listen up. As we all know, any tragedy represents a conflict between two truths. In our situation here, we're dealing with one truth, that the destruction of a human life is the most brutal form of power, and another, competing truth, that life itself is the most brutal, most extreme form of power, because no human being comes into the world of his own volition. No one asked you or me if we wanted to be born. We're born, we grow up and live because others made that decision on our behalf. Therefore the greatest act of resistance an anti-authoritarian could commit is to end his life, and to end his life of his own volition, since life itself is the most violent form of power. Consequently, the only true anti-authoritarian isn't just a dead anti-authoritarian, but one who died by suicide. And yet the destruction of life, as we've already established,

- 113 -

is also the most violent form of power. Therefore the true anti-authoritarian, who's realized that resistance to power is an ontological act and that he bears no relation to those ignorant fools who think resistance means painting an A in a circle on a wall or throwing Molotov cocktails at the cops or smashing shop windows and banks – our fine, upstanding anti-authoritarian isn't the victim of a tragedy, or even the protagonist of the greatest tragedy unfolding every hour and every minute in the universe, but rather is an embodiment of tragedy, an embodied tragedy. Because in order to abolish the most brutal form of power, life, he has to exercise the most brutal form of power, the destruction of life. Quod erat demonstrandum. Or something like that.

Sir, sir.

What is it now?

Sorry, but you lost us. Can you start over from the beginning?

Of course I lost you. The Greek family and the Greek school system are twin wombs of evil. You were born from one and reborn in the other. How on earth could you possibly understand? Now go out and smash a shop window or two, smoke a joint, knock back a few beers to the health of the revolution and the memory of Alexis Grigoropoulos. Just make sure you're not late getting home, because your mother is making pork chops with fried potatoes and they'll get cold. Yeah, don't be late getting back home sweet home, because mommy made a nice little dinner and you don't want it to get cold.

You're going to do it, though, aren't you, sir? You'll do it in the end, whatever you say. We know you will.

What?

You know what. You'll do it in the end. You're a good person. And alone. And kind of crazy. Those three go together.

A good person? What does that mean? And who cares? What matters isn't whether you're good, but whether you love.

A good person is someone who does good, who does the right thing. A good person is someone who's stopped wondering why he has to do good. That's what a good person is. See, sir? We know a thing or two. We're not just dumb bricks. There's more to us than just smashing windows, then running home and eating our nice little pork chops and fried potatoes. We know a thing or two ourselves.

Tap tap tap.

Chronis rolls his wheelchair in reverse and goes over to the desk again. He breaks off a piece of bread and dips it in the wine and rolls another little coin and tosses it into the tank. This time the scorpion doesn't wait at all but rushes toward the bread before it even lands on the broken rooftile.

Tap tap tap, Chronis taps his finger against the glass.

Take, eat; this is my body, Chronis says.

Drink of it, all of you, this is my blood.

Amen.

—∞—

Night is falling. Night has fallen. Any minute now the procession will pass by. Listen to the bells. It's coming. Or maybe not? The procession is later than usual this year. And the girl – she's late, too, very late coming out of the old man's room.

Chronis maneuvers the wheelchair like a captain on open waters – reverse, hold there, ninety to the left, wheel to center, straight ahead calmly, hold, ninety to the right, wheel to center, straight on from there – then goes out into the hallway, stops outside the closed door, leans over and puts his ear to the keyhole. Between the tolling of the bells he can hear his mother snoring – he did a good job again tonight with his special caipillinha cocktail, she knocked it back and is sleeping the good sleep, I should've been a bartender after all, hush over there, don't raise a scare, don't knock on the door, what's that pounding for, mommy dearest is sleeping, nani nani nani nani, and if she's hurt it'll make her well, hush dear mother in your walnut shell, in your pearly clothes, the tiniest belle, hush dear child, where are you going, I'm going to the farmer, for cheese to grate by the kitchen gate, and pinches and kisses all the way home – Chronis leaves his mother, goes into the kitchen and takes the knife from the drawer, then wheels back into the hallway, stops in front of the mirror, puts the knife in his mouth, and bites down on the blade – watch out, don't get carried away, don't get too cocky, this knife is your goal – and he sees his hair mussed in the mirror, sticking up like a squad of soldiers whom a siren startled from sleep, oh Hamlet, poor Hamlet, it was the wrong question, the wrong place, the wrong time, it's not to be or not to be, it's how to be, and if you were here now that's what you'd be asking, if you were here now, on this island, in this country that isn't a ghost but a figment of the imagination – because to be a ghost means you were once alive, and this country never lived at all, it never existed, it was all a lie, a fairytale with a crooked beginning and completely warped ending, oh poor Hamlet, you think Denmark is a prison – but if you were here now, poor Hamlet, you'd know what a prison really is, if you were standing in front of this mirror, you'd agree that fathers and mirrors should be hated to an equal degree because they alone have the ability to make people multiply.

Or something like that.

Teeth clenching the knife, Chronis pushes the wheelchair forward – a maestro in the chair but his cock won't crow – and when he reaches the front door he opens it and looks both ways up and down the street. He has to hurry. He has to cross the street quickly, the procession will be there any minute. He has to hurry, the procession is almost there. Listen to the church-bells. Dtin dtan dtin dtan, the bells toll. Hey, man, who died? A wounded cat. Who wounded it? I did, and I brought it to the doctor and he gave it fat, and the cat told him, I won't eat that. And he gave it stew and it said, thank you. He has to hurry. He has to hurry. He takes the knife from his mouth and licks his lips. Salt and blood. Salt and rust. For months he's had the same taste in his mouth – salt from the sea, the rust of blood. Naturalism, someone might say. Cheap words, out of cheap mouths, out of cheap minds. Out of cheap hearts. Naturalism, sure. Come live here for a while and then we'll talk. Come live here, not as a tourist in August, not camping in Echo Bay, not as a bartender for three months in tourist season or as an army conscript for six, not for cocaine and joints and drinks and dancing, or bonfires at night, guitars and singing on the beach, orgies in the moonlight, empty conversations with empty friends and empty girls about the empty revolution – come here in November when the sirocco whips up the sand and listen to the gulls screeching like rabid dogs, come when the west wind blows at forty knots, sweeping into the harbor like a wild beast and crushing everything in its path, come see the lightning on March nights, flashing white in the sky like ghosts over the masts of boats, come when it's raining on silent yellow evenings and walk through the town, through the narrow streets, see the little houses, the little shops, the little people, come then, and you'll figure out fast enough how easy it is, if you live here, to become a little person yourself.

Come and live here for a while, and you'll learn to wonder and doubt. And I don't mean you'll remember, or relearn. You'll learn. You'll learn to see and to believe. You'll learn to believe in things you can't see. And then you'll see the things you believe in. Come live here. Here where we came to live, on this island, in the middle of this sea, we have to write the world all over again from the beginning. Not my life or your life, just life – that's what we have to write again from the beginning. We have to write the earth, the sea, darkness and light, language and silence, sleep, dreams, passion, death, love. The city is a trap and a trap means safety. The terror of the sea is stronger than the pain of that trap, the pain of a heart attack, the pain of kidney stones. Come and look terror straight in the eye – because that terror may redeem us. Come and learn to love fear, because that's the only way you'll stop being afraid. Kill the ancient man you have inside. He who fears the gods fears all things, says Plutarch, earth and sea, air and sky, darkness and light, sound and silence, and a dream. Kill him. He's not your father, you're not his son. You're strangers. You're a foreigner, a guard in someone else's house. And a useless guard at that, whose veins run with bile, not blood – I'm not well, so the whole world can go to hell. Only when you come to believe that this house isn't yours, will this house become yours.

Tap tap tap. The scorpion is writhing in the tank. Tap tap tap. It ate the flesh and drank the blood, and now it wants another coin, more flesh, more blood. The scorpion is hungry, the scorpion is thirsty, it strikes its pincers on the rocks, strikes the glass with its tail, strikes and strikes. Tap tap tap.

Don't be scared, Chronis says to the scorpion. Don't be scared.

Kill the German, Chronis hears his father saying. Not me, the German. You hear? The German's the one to kill. Don't count days. Don't count kilometers. All you need to count is how many Germans you kill. You hear me? Chronis? That's my boy, Chronis, my brave boy. But what happened to you? Why are you in that wheelchair, Chronis?

It's not a wheelchair, Chronis says. It's a mobility device. Stress on the biii-ing and the ice. Mo *biiii* lity dev *iiiice*.

Chronis looks around. He looks between the leaves of the mulberry tree and under the iron table in the yard, where the wasps have made a nest again, looks past the flagless flagpole in the corner, next to the pots of basil, rosemary, mint, looks here, looks there – see, pal, what too much tragedy can do to a person, too much pity, too much fear – and then his gaze falls on a yellow bug with crushed legs struggling over the cement in the yard – see, pal, the kind of insignificant things a man notices at the height of panic – and then he raises the hand that's holding the knife and slashes it through the air with brusque, nimble movements.

Beware, old mole, Chronis yells. Beware of my sharp and supple sword, lest it dice you like an onion. O father, unnerved father, beware, lest you find yourself splayed on the ground, vomiting up your soul, your murdered blood spurting into the air as I watch with closed eyes and the black spatter refreshes me. Get lost. Crawl back into your hole, you old rat. You're no king and I'm no prince and my mother isn't going to drink poisoned wine. Sure, it's true, I mixed her a pretty killer cocktail tonight. Caipillinha number two. It's a stiff one, with those Seroxat 30 mg pills. It's really something. And the mother will drink and the child dare not, yet.

Chronis, son, what are you talking about? Have you gone mad?

No, Dad, but I have gone bad. Bad as in curdled, like spoiled milk. In this house time just refuses to pass. There's nothing on TV, the internet is always on the fritz, so what can I do but read and read, like there's no tomorrow. I went to town on Sophocles, Aeschylus, and Shakespeare. They're a tough crowd, that's for sure. Anyhow, what's new with you? What's happening up there? You guys must have a lot on your plate these days, huh?

Chronis, is that a knife you're carrying? Where are you going with that knife?

To hell, and with a handbasket, too. To gather greens for the Easter feast. We'll make kokoretsi out of wild asparagus. We'll eat till we burst, pop. I bet you guys up there don't roast lamb, do you? Makes sense, why would the chief want to see his little brothers roasting on the spit? Well, I should get going. I have to hurry, the procession will be passing by any minute.

Chronis rolls his wheelchair forward and opens the garden gate. A wind has picked up and from up there on the hill he can see the lights flickering down at the harbor and further off the lighthouse at Fonias that goes on and off twice every ten seconds. He stops and times it just to make sure. Good, it's still going, two in ten. Some things in this world are still running on time. That's something, at least. It's a comfort, for sure. Two in ten. Yep. Two in ten.

Chronis?

Pop?

Chronis, I said.

Pop, I said.

Why are your eyes like that, Chronis? Son? Chron-akis. Your eyes are so dark and red, and as big as a cow's. What's wrong, my boy?

It's nothing, dad. Though you're right, I'm going for the bull's-eye view, trying to take livestock of the situation. And you know what I see? I see the best minds of my generation destroyed. Not by LSD but by LSJ. Short for life-sucking joblessness. They overdosed on LSJ. Get it, Dad? LSJ, a little patent of my own. You like it? It's a neologism. Or maybe a neoplasm. Words are cancer down here on this island, they corrode my brain a little bit every day, my tongue, my heart. A psychic edema where I'd prefer some psychedelica. But seriously, Dad, they've all lost their minds. They burned out, overdosed, they're ruined. I try my best to be a good listener over the phone but the wind drowns them out. A north wind or a west wind, it makes no difference, any kind of wind just carries their voices away. Remember Anna, Dad? Remember how you used to sit on the balcony in summer and close your eyes and listen to her practicing and the sound was like a lullaby rocking you to sleep? Remember that? Well, Anna sold the piano, the only time she plays these days is at Hantoumis's patisseries, a euro per trill, she wears a jacket and a bow tie and a little name tag, because Chopin sweetens the baklava, profiteroles taste better with Beethoven. And Aris, LSJ fucked him up, too, they canned everyone from the furniture factory, then hired them back off the books as day laborers, no benefits, but at least he had some money coming in, except the other day he got into a fight with another guy about who was going to assemble a dining room table, the other guy said he should get the job because he'd been there longer, and one thing led to another and before you know it Aris pulls a screwdriver out of his back pocket and starts chasing him around in the street, so now Aris lost even that daily wage, because the boss said, I don't want thugs in my shop, and of course he's right because a screwdriver is for screwing things together, not for ripping people's guts out, and in the difficult times our nation is currently experiencing we all have to keep calm and optimistic, present a united front, we've got business plans to pursue, and balance sheets and operating costs and inelastic expenses, and while wages can be made as elastic as rubber bands, stretched as thin as ice, as butter over too much bread, expenses can't, people may lie but numbers always tell the truth, and besides, chasing people around in the streets with screwdrivers certainly isn't going to help, what kind of crap is that, anyhow, where on earth is this country headed, what are we, living in a jungle or something? Remember Rita, Dad? Well, the dentist fired her six months ago and she's been poring over the help wanted ads ever since, calling around every day, and the last time we talked she says to me, listen to this,

I call this one number and a Nigerian guy answers and tells me he's a stripper for bachelorette parties in the northern suburbs and says, I'll give you twenty euros for every gig you book, and asks what I did before, and I say dental assistant and he says cool, fine, so you know how to deal with phone calls and bookings, come on, he says, don't think twice, there's money in it, and potential, too. And you know what Rita says to me, Dad? She says, man, you know what I want? You know what I want more than anything? I want this whole country to disappear off the map. To shrink to a tiny tiny tiny speck and then to fucking vanish off the map, to just cease to exist. That's what I want, that's it. For this whore of a country to disappear off the map forever. Dad. Are you listening? Are you still there, Dad, or are you gone?

Chronis, he hears his dad saying. Where are you going with that knife?

Chronis looks at the knife, then grips it tightly in his hand and shivers. It's already May, but it's freezing again tonight. Thirty degrees in the daytime, fifteen at night. Or twelve. Or ten. Hot, then cold. Expansion, contraction. Constant distortion. How much can the body stand, or the heart, the mind?

Crick crack, Chronis is expanding.

Crick crack, Chronis is contracting.

Crick crack, the chasm in Chronis spreads.

Well, Dad, Chronis says, I thought I'd run across the street and see what's going on, something's not right tonight. I'll park in front of the stairs and go up and see what's happening in that room. He hasn't done this sort of thing before, hasn't had her in there for so many hours. The old man, I mean. It's the first time he's locked her in there for so long. You don't know her. If you saw her you'd understand. Like a doll. Soft blond fuzz. A body that glows like a candle in church. If you saw her you'd understand. The old geezer sure did. And ever since, he's been trying to turn that candle into a rubber band. I don't know if you get my meaning. If you can fathom the unfathomable, hear the unheard of, comprehend the incomprehensible. Anyhow, I'm going to climb up and see what's going on. Because the procession will be here any minute now. I'm going to pull myself up the stairs like a worm, get myself into that room and see what's going on. What's taking so long. I have to go and see. Rubber-band-girl to worm-man, over. Rubber-band-girl to worm-man, over. Mayday. Mayday.

Mayday. Who's going to drive you home tonight? Chronis with all his might. And his is nothing to sniff at, that's for sure. His might, that is. His you-know-what, too, if you catch my drift. It's a big one, but fallen in action. But don't worry, we'll get it back up. Oh, yes. We'll raise the dead there, too. Resurrections all around. Science can work wonders these days. Pumps, rings, injections. Have you heard of Alprostadil? It's a miracle drug. Viagra for cripples. Sorry, I mean people with special needs. Sorry, I mean people with special abilities. We'll have him fighting on the front lines again in no time, all the former cripples carrying the banner of a new Greece. We'll raise the dead there, too, no doubt about it. We'll pump the bastard up, no question. No question. Sorry, Dad, I got carried away. Let myself just float down the river a while. What can we do, it's all part of life.

Chronis?

Dad?

I wish I could die twice. I wish I could take you in my arms and lift you up, even if I had to die a second time. I wouldn't care. Just to see you stand on your feet again. I'd die twice over to see that, or three times, even. To be able to squeeze your hands, son, to hold you in my arms and lift you to your feet. Nothing else, just that. Then I'd gladly die again. Just that.

Beat it, old man. Beat it or I'll beat you. Get thee behind me, pops. Enough with the lamentation, or you'll die not twice but a hundred and thrice. Come on, Dad, don't cry. Let's sing some marching songs together, or recite some heroic poems about a worm-man advancing toward his fate with open eyes and sealed lips, I walk through the snow, burning up, and in the fire I freeze, a cloud gathers above, sign of winter, as I stand here imprisoned obeying the words within, fire is fire, my heart is broke, but I have some glue, that's how the final acts in life are written, let's get drunk on an immortal cocktail of postmodernism and multiculturalism, post-structuralism and intertextuality, one shot Alexandrou, one shot Cobain, another of Archilochus, a Carnation jingle and a little Nietzsche, a Xanax and a dash of Grig-orios Nissis, mix some Plutarch with a bit of Borges, some Ehrenburg with Vamvakaris, some reader response with psychotropic response and of course some govern-ment response to the plight of the unemployed – I should've been a bartender after all, Chronis says, and puts the knife in his mouth and rolls the wheelchair into the street, not looking back, let the dead bury the dead – Chronis moves forward, not looking back, not hearing his father's death rattle behind him, or his mother's snoring, or the rattling of the scorpion who by now has stopped tapping the glass with its black tail and instead is thrusting it into a tawny body as unfeeling as a shadow, again and again, manically, frenziedly the scorpion stings its own pallid body, a body sated on flesh and blood.

Rubber-band-girl to worm-man, over.

Rubber-band-girl to worm-man.

Over.

Mayday. Mayday. Mayday.

Chronis quickly crosses the street and stops beneath the fig tree where the other day someone spread too much potash and dried it out, probably killed it. He stops, out of breath, and looks at the dry branches rising into the crucified sky, branches like fingers that never had a chance to become fists but petrified there in an ambiguous, tribiguous, tripartite gesture, dry fingers rising into the sky seeking revenge, forgiveness, relief.

Ethics comes from ethos, and ethos means abode, dwelling place, Chronis says, staring at the branches, struggling to see the stars through the branches. That's what the gloomster from Messkirch said, but let's not rush to kill him just yet. If ethos is an abode, then a change of abode entails a change of ethos. Take the island. The island messes with everything. You came to live here, so now you have to change your moral code. No, that's not right. Now that you live here, the island's ethics will change you. The place will change you. The dark horse from Ephesus put it differently, that a man's character is his fate, and Mr. Gloom and Doom from Elsinore said an awful sickness can only be awfully healed, and the gloomy guy from Röcken said knowledge kills action. Knowledge blunts the knife.

Or something like that.

Chronis looks down the street. There's been a change to the route, the procession won't be passing by any minute, or anytime soon. Change in the program, the procession won't be coming at all. And the bells. Either I've gone deaf or the bells have lost their voice. A change of moral code, change of place. The island messes with everything.

Rubber-band-girl to worm-man.

Rubber-band-girl to worm-man.

Nah, don't listen to any of those pussies, a woman doesn't have three holes, the old geezer says at the coffee house. A woman has as many holes as you make. You can shove it in her nostril if you want, and give her brain a good mix. But you've got to start on the nostrils when they're young if you want to knock any sense into them.

Mayday. Mayday. Mayday.

He pivots his chair, pulls up in front of the stairs, and looks up at the room. Lights off, curtains drawn. Courage, man. Courage, Chronis. Courage, my boy. Blessed be those with crippled legs who refuse to let their hearts be crippled, too. But what a tragedy. The church has no room for real Christians. And those capable of changing the world aren't of this world, don't belong here. Be brave, Chronis. Take courage. Don't listen to the other foreigners – good will come from the sea not in a rowboat or on a ship, but in a floating wheelchair. Make your hair into sails, your hands into oars – row, row, even if the wind pushes you backwards. Be brave, Chronis. Don't let the sweat dry. Don't let your heart dry up, either. Don't let your hand dry up, or the knife. Courage. Courage. Our life and our death are with our neighbor. Choose one of the two, so the two become one. Courage, Chronis. Be brave. Don't let Chronis dry up.

Chronis reaches out a hand and grabs hold of the handrail beside the stairs. Green, hard, rough, it scrapes his skin. You can do this. Be brave, Chronis. Never trust the artist, trust the tale. You can do this. Courage.

He puts the knife in his mouth and bites the blade and grips the handrail with both hands, grips the green metal as tightly as he can, and with all the strength in his half a body he leans forward and slips out of the wheelchair. He falls face-down against the edge of a step, but doesn't feel the pain. He feels no pain at all. He's already sweating. One, two, three, twenty. Twenty steps. A challenge, a trial like no other. Saint Chronis of the Staircase. Saint Chronis the Paraplegic. The Holy Servant of the Wheelchair. Twenty steps. Courage. Hold onto that metal in your hand, that steel in your mouth. Hold onto the sweat that will drip drops of blood on the cement.

He grips the handrail between his hands and the blade between his teeth and starts to pull himself up the stairs. It's good, it's good. It's good he's carrying only half a body, he can't feel the other half at all. He's climbing. Not crawling, climbing. Step by step, no matter how long it takes, how much he sweats, how much pain still awaits.

I'm coming, Chronis whispers, staring straight at the sky which stares back at him with its two billion eyes.

I'm coming, he whispers and feels his blood sweetening where the steel bites his tongue.

I'm coming, Chronis says.

I'm coming.

Our island is expanding. Last year, after the series of earthquakes started up, Germans and Swiss came from the University of Hamburg and the Swiss Institute of Technology and installed seismographs and special GPS machines up on the mountain, in Doors and around the lakes and apparently discovered that the island, which is hollow, is moving in three different directions at a speed of 70 millimeters a year: toward the northwest, the northeast and the southeast. They also discovered that it isn't moving only horizontally but vertically as well – in Doors, along the edge of the largest plate, the activity of the magma under the surface is pushing the land up about three centimeters a year. They even found that there had been about two hundred earthquakes in a single year, most under four on the Richter scale, and that large quantities of radon are escaping from the trench that opened last winter, over in Mougkros, and that the island is ringed by three underground volcanoes in addition to Kamenes – two between Moray Bay and Murderess and one behind Barbarian Isle.

Today my father is all mixed up again. That's how it's been going these days, one day he's pretty bad, the next he's even worse. He woke me up before dawn to tell me to go into town and buy a radon meter. A radon meter, sure. Fine, I said, but why go all the way into town? Anna has stuff like that at the mini-market, I'll bring you one when I go for cigarettes. I mean, I shouldn't say stuff like that, because he realizes I'm making fun of him and he gets upset and looks at me with eyes brimming with tears, but sometimes my frustration gets the better of me. He says we need to measure the radon levels in the house and take the necessary steps to protect ourselves, the situation has gotten dangerous – we're talking radon here, it's no laughing matter. Twenty thousand people die every year in America from radon poisoning, and just as many in Europe.

He woke me up at six to tell me this. We fought, we shouted, I tried being harsh, I tried being gentle, but it was all wasted effort.

Bring me some clothes so I can get dressed and I'll go myself, he says. I want my striped shirt and khaki shots. No way I'm wearing long pants, it's too hot.

Shots, I say, and give him a good look. You want to wear shots.

Definitely, he says. The khaki ones, with the big pockets.

At some point I thought I about calling Pothitos, but I thought better of it, what could I say and how could he help? Ioanna, dear, I'm a neurologist – as for matters of radon and other radioactive materials you'll have to call over to the research foundation, or the Committee on Nuclear Energy. That's what he'll say, for sure, and I'll just laugh. And my father will hear from his room and bow his head and get all teary again.

Eventually, with this and that, I managed to calm him down. I told him I'd only take him into town if he took his pills first, and fortunately he swallowed them without any fuss and fortunately they did their job and fortunately now he's asleep.

But not for long. Not for long, I know.

Soon enough he'll jump up again and grab me by the arm and tell me not to go out tonight. Don't leave, he'll say. I don't want to have to wander around in the middle of nowhere shouting your name. Ioanna, Ioanna, where are you? I'm telling you, if you go out, I'll die. Tonight, I mean it.

Cross my heart, look.

If you leave, tonight is the night I'll die.

Good Will Come from the Sea

Peeetrooos!
Petraaaakiiis!
Where are you?

Lazaros the Bow drops his walking stick and flashlight and falls to his knees and presses his ear to the dry earth. He holds his breath, closes his eyes, and struggles to hear something, the twin dogs of fear and worry nipping wildly at his chest. Eyes shut, holding his breath, he waits to hear something. Not something, someone. Not someone, Petros. If Petros went into the Dragon Cave that night and if the cave stretches, as they say, whole kilometers beneath the island, and if the island is, as they say, hollow in places, then at some point he'll surely be able to hear him.

Surely, at some point he'll hear him.

Surely, there's no other way.

He kneels there for a while, almost entirely still, whispering the same word over and over like a prayer, whispering the prayer of the one and only word.

Petros. Petros. Petros.

Then, rising to his feet, stumbling heavily, he braces himself on the walking stick, hunched over, his other hand gripping the flashlight, which he aims at the sky like a mad warrior from some fairy tale who got it in his mind that tonight is the night to spear the moon with his sword.

He leans back with his eyes closed and breathes in deeply through his nose, then shouts at the top of his lungs, with all the strength he has left.

Peeetrooos!

Petraaaaakis!

His mouth loves his son's name.

The moon has cycled through five colors tonight. It rose bright red out of the sea, off in the distance behind Inner Island, then faded to orange, then went yellow over the peak of Polemos, Mount War, then silver over Outer

Island, and finally, around midnight, when it started to whiten like a blind man's eye, Lazaros the Bow splashed his face with cold water to sober up and, as every night, pulled on his leather Meindl Taiga hunting boots, waterproof and weighing less than a kilo, made of breathable GORE-TEX fabric and soft, comfortable memory foam, with Air-Active inserts and Multigriff natural rubber soles, then his durable Deerhunter waterproof hunting pants and two-tone Beretta vest with the hidden pockets and shell pouches in front, and then strapped his hunting knife, a double-edged KA-BAR – which, as everyone knows, can ward off evil things – tightly to his leg, and slung his pistol – which, as everyone knows, can ward off evil people – crosswise under his arm, and feeling strong and capable, as if he were wearing a full suit of armor, he takes the flashlight and the walking stick – also durable, carved from abelitsia, curved and knotted – and hurriedly leaves the house, before dawn on All Souls' Day, June seventh, with the whitewashed houses of the town glistening in the moonlight, tumbling from the castle at the top of the hill all the way down to the sea, like the frothing waters of the rushing Hiona in winter.

Tonight Lazaros decided to go a different way. He'll follow the moonlight, head west, to Outer Island, hugging the coastline all the way to Second Coming, then circle the lake and come back through Murderer's Gorge, and before he reaches Beast's Hole turn north and head toward Mougkros. He's never taken this route by foot before but figures he should get to the Dragon Cave by dawn, in time to see the sun rising out of the sea — he wants to be sure he's there in time to see daybreak from up above the cave, because that sort of thing is a sign, it's a good sign to see a day dawn, and besides, sunlight brings a ray of hope — no matter how much darkness you're carrying with you, inside of you, sunlight always offers a ray of hope — and as that kook Charonis said the other day at the taverna, we should believe in the sun not only because we see it, but because it's what lets us see everything else.

It's no small thing, running a taverna. There's no end to what you can learn. You just have to keep your eyes and ears open. And all the time, too, not just to check on orders, bills, customers, waiters. So nothing escapes you, so you notice everything, hear everything people say between the pear and the cheese, as they say. Or the

Heineken and moussakas, the ouzo and sardines.

Leaving the last houses of the town behind, just before he turns onto the road for Seven Threshing Floors, he stops at Mute's Spring to fill his canteen. He sticks his head under the flow and lets the water carve his skin, countless blades slicing into the nape of his neck, into his temples and ears.

Hey there, Lazaros. Whatcha doin, poor devil, he soon hears a voice asking him.

What do you think I'm doing, Lazaros says out loud, without looking around. I'm waiting to sober up so I can get pissed again.

From the low wall where he's sitting, by the spring, he can see the ruined castle at the top of the hill and the Church of the Butchered Virgin, which tonight, in the half dark, shines white like a seashell that ancient waves carried to the top of the black rock. As he sits there with crossed legs and rolls a cigarette – the last cigarette of the waning night, first of the dawning day – he looks at the hazy outline up there and feels two cold hands creeping over his back and gripping him by the shoulders – you know, Petrakis, they say in the old days that filthy dog Canum Hoca sat up there in the castle, cutting his tobacco with a scimitar on an icon of the Virgin Mary. That's why they call her the Butchered Virgin. To this day, if you look close you can still see the marks on the wood. There are wounds like that all over this island, Petrakis. Saracens, Franks, Venetians, Turks, pirates, Italians, Germans – wounds from so many knives. But the deepest ones, the ones that hurt the most, are the ones we made ourselves. A brother's knife cuts twice as deep as a stranger's. And we're still at it today.

He smokes his cigarette, then stubs it out on the edge of the low wall, takes a last look at the church, and rises to his feet. He puts the canteen in the right pocket of his vest – the other one is already occupied by a flask of tsikoudia – picks up his flashlight and walking stick and sets off down the dirt road, eyes trained on the soil, speaking to Petros, whom he imagines walking with him now, beside him – because he'd like that so much, he'd like more than anything in the world to have his son beside him tonight, and it's no small thing to hear a human voice in the darkness, it's a comfort, a great comfort, even if the voice is only your own.

Wounds from so many knives, my boy. So many.

Once we were divided into right and left, now we have foreigners and rats. A handful of people on a handful of soil, doing our best to exterminate one another. Here we are in the twenty-first century, still hunting each other down. This place is crumbling, everything's in ruins, but here we still are, knife to knife, wound after wound. We foreigners on one side, rats on the other. So now our evil is added to theirs, added to the pile. And you know what's to blame, Petrakis? The fact that we never really loved this place. Never. People talk about pride. Sure, I'm proud to be a Greek. But what good is pride, really? Pride is a tree with rotten roots: if the wind blows, it falls. What we need is love. You have to love your land, feel for it, that's what matters. And since we never truly loved this place, soon enough we came to truly hate it. That's precisely what happened. There may be such a thing as false love, but there's no such thing as false hate. Which is why we now hate this place to death. Most of all the young folk, the kids, the new generation they're always talking about. Not you, Petros. Not you, my boy, you don't have a drop of hatred in your whole body. I'm talking about the others, not you. Petros, Petrakis, my brave boy, my light.. I mean the others, not you.

Lazaros walks with his eyes trained on the ground and as he moves, they, too, move over the ground.

The other day at the taverna someone was saying how when you're young, you plan for the future, and when you're old, you're nostalgic for the past. So the whole joy of life disappears, the joy of the here and now. Feeling nostalgic for the past, planning for the future. Planning for the past, feeling nostalgic for the future. Today gets caught in a vise between tomorrow and yesterday, and it writhes and dies. You listening? I sure hope you're listening.

Talk fueled by wine, tsikoudia, ouzo. But Lazaros likes listening to talk like that. His mind is a sponge, it absorbs everything. That's why he drinks. To keep the sponge moist, so it can absorb even better, even more. So nothing goes wasted. And whatever it soaks up, he later squeezes back out into his son's sponge, which of course is still small and shapeless, the pores haven't yet opened wide. But they will, in time. That's what love is. Someone else might say, I love my child, I don't care about myself, everything I do I do for my child. I want to see my kid succeed in the world, so I can be proud of him. That's nonsense. If you don't love yourself, how are you going to love your child? If you don't love what you are, how can you love what you're not? This is old news, Christ has been saying it for two thousand years, but people can't get it through their thick skulls. Christ didn't say, love your neighbor instead of yourself. He said, love your neighbor as yourself. And he was right. If you don't love yourself, there's no way you'll ever love anyone at all – not even your own child. If you don't have ambitions of your own, how can you have ambitions for your kids? If you don't accomplish anything in your life, how do you expect your kids to accomplish anything in theirs? Poor bastard, poor fool. Of course you might ask what I've accomplished, talking the big talk. But I've done a thing or two. Just the fact that I was father and mother to that boy all these years, it's no small thing. And the fact that I came with nothing to this snake pit and within a few years managed to stand on my own two feet – doesn't that count for something? Besides, even if I hadn't done anything at all, I still wouldn't be like them. Because I've got knowledge, see? I know who I am and where I stand and how to raise my child. I've got eyes and ears. I've got eyes and ears all over.

I'm not someone who has the mouth of a lion and the heart of a fly. No, I've got the heart of a lion and the mouth of a fly.

There's a big difference.

See?

⸭

Lazaros walks with his eyes trained on the ground, feeling other eyes on him – like a fiend from a fairy tale, tonight the darkness has sprouted a thousand staring eyes – and when he reaches the straightaway where the Doors begin, the narrow stretch of land that joins Inner to Outer Island, Lower to Upper Part, Big to Little Handcuff, he steps off the road and goes to stand at the very edge of that awful cliff and looks down at the sea spreading to the right and left, looks at the waves tipped with white like frothy eyebrows over the water's countless blind eyes, and far off in the distance, the flickering lights from other islands, which send silent signs again tonight – hazy, mysterious messages.

Peeetrooos!

Petraaaakiiis!

He makes his hands into a cone and shouts. He shouts with all the strength in his body, shouts until his voice drowns out the whine of the north wind that seems to carry other, strange voices from far away, moans, howls from mouths that seem hardly human. He shouts until he feels his chest burn, the veins in his neck swelling, the blood becoming one with his phlegm and sticking in his throat like a rock.

He bends over and coughs, his whole body shaking, coughing so hard he starts to sweat. A wild, cutting cough, the wheezing bark of an asthmatic dog.

He wipes his mouth with his sleeve, takes deep breaths. He waits. He looks ahead, gaze blurred, unseeing, and waits.

And then he straightens up and cups his hands around his mouth again.

Peeetrooos!

Petraaaaakiiis!

Can you hear me?

So last summer, two old ladies come into the restaurant, tourists. Petros goes over to take their order, they open the menu and start in on a whole slew of questions, what's this, what's that. I'm sitting off to one side watching him and I can see he's starting to get all worked up. I mean, it's one of his first days on the job and he still hasn't gotten used to the idea, he's all grumbling and resentment. I don't say anything, I figure I'll wait and see what happens. So the old ladies order, I don't know, a salad and a tzatziki, then turn to the main courses. I see them examine the menu, whisper to one another, look back at the menu, whisper some more, then they ask the kid something and he leans over to look, too, and one of the ladies points up at the light fixture on the ceiling. And the kid turns bright red and says, no, no, no lamp, laaamb, laaamb, you know, baaa, baaa. The old ladies start laughing and say, OK, OK, and Petros picks up the menus and comes over all in a huff and asks me who wrote the English menu.

Sifis, I say, from Miramare next door. Why?

Tell that blockhead, he says, that the animal that goes baaa, baaa is spelled with a b in English, not a p. Those old bats thought we were going to serve them a plate of roast lamp with potatoes. We look like fools.

Lazaros the Bow remembers the whole scene all over again as he looks down at the lights of the port from up in Agioupes – he remembers how his son flushed bright red that afternoon and how he'd tried to keep from laughing, flaring his nostrils, until both of them suddenly burst into laughter at once – just imagine, roast lamp with potatoes – and threw their arms around one another's shoulders, laughing under the grape arbor, and Lazaros remembers how he hugged his son, couldn't get his fill, felt his own unshaven cheek grazing his child's soft neck, and the hair stood up on his arms as he squeezed the kid's bony ribs – how strange it is, to have the hair to stand up on your arms as you touch flesh that came from your flesh – and he remembers them later, telling the others in the kitchen the story about the old ladies, and they all laughed together, laughed until they cried, just imagine, lamp with potatoes, Lazaros remembers it all tonight and smiles and feels like laughing the way he did that afternoon last summer, laughing until he cries.

He remembers it all again tonight, Lazaros the Bow. He remembers another night, too, a few months later, when Drakakis came in with a pack of whores in miniskirts up to their navels and Lazaros seated them at the best table and served them a spotted grouper that weighed seven and a half kilos, as big as a baby, and watched as the plates of crayfish kept coming, and scallops and sea figs, and he poured more and more champagne and wine – bring it on, Drakakis kept saying, fish should be eaten fresh, and money spent fresh, too – and then near dawn Lazaros sat down at the table, and called Petros over, too, this here is my son, and this is Mr. Haris Drakakis, the shipowner. Petros sat down beside him and looked at the blondes cackling like geese and Drakakis pulled some cigars out of his pocket and handed one to each of them, cigars as big as stove-pipes, and poured them some wine and they all clinked glasses and Lazaros told his son to tell the story about the old ladies and the lamp and Drakakis laughed so hard he almost fell off his chair, then grabbed Petros by the shoulders and told him to keep talking, keep the laughter coming. Lazaros watched his son talk, the cigar perched between two of Petros's fingers, and watched Drakakis laugh, chewing on his own cigar with drooping lids, and Lazaros wondered what it would be like to have money, lots of money, to be a kid not even thirty years old and have more money than the next guy will make in thirty lives put together, to own half an island, to have new women every week, a new car every month, a new yacht every year. Money, piles of money. To hop on your yacht and sail off to Mykonos for an afternoon swim, then to Santorini for dinner. A week later Drakakis came back to the taverna and wanted Petros to tell some more stories so they could laugh. The week after that he called him to the yacht, and they started hanging out a lot, until two or three months later he offered him a job as a driver for the Piraeus offices, a thousand for his first month's salary, all expenses paid. Petros didn't want to go – he doesn't want a driver, he wants a clown, he told his father. But Lazaros pressured him into it, he wasn't about to let an opportunity like that go wasted.

You're going, he said. Others in your position would kill for a job like that. This is the Drakakises we're dealing with, they own the whole island. We're talking buckets of money, this isn't just small fry. You can't turn him down. Whenever he comes to the taverna his bill is ten times the size of anyone else's. But that's not the issue. The issue is, a wide road is opening before you. A road paved with money. You're going. I won't let my son end up a taverna owner. You're going.

There's something else, too, Petros said. The guy

wants me —

There's nothing else, Lazaros said. You're going. You have to go. Not for me, but for yourself. For your own good.

You're going.

You're going, end of story.

———— ⬥ ————

Money. The alpha and the omega. Where everything begins and where everything ends. All the rest is small print. And whoever won't admit it is a fool or a liar. That's why poor people are eternally cursed. Because they don't hate money, only those who have it. They hate money not because it exists, but because it isn't theirs. That's why they're cursed forever, that's why they'll never gain any power. Because what they want isn't to stop being poor, but to be rich.

Lazaros walks with his eyes trained on the ground and as he moves, they too move over the ground. He walks with his head bent, feeling other eyes watching him — once again the night is full of eyes, so many eyes, countless eyes — and when he reaches the crossroads at Daidala he stops to catch his breath, take a swig of tsikoudia, and smoke a cigarette.

Money. Ever since Petros was a kid, when he was old enough to understand, he'd tried to teach him to love money. Love money, don't be afraid of it. Money is a part of you, just remember that. Like your heart, like your arms and legs, that's how money is, too. A part of you. Can you live without a heart? If you had to choose whether or not to have arms, what would you choose? That's how money is, too. Like your heart, your arms, your legs. You have to have money. Are you listening? You can't live without money. There's no point in living.

Love money. Care for it. Love it the way you love your arms and your legs, your eyes, your ears. Don't listen to those idiots who say it doesn't matter whether or not you have money. It's like saying that having two arms is the same as having one arm or none at all. Don't listen to those people. Love money. Love it, don't be afraid of it. Whoever hates money hates himself. And whoever hates himself hates the whole world. That hatred is something poor people cultivate. It's what a blind man feels for a man who can see, a paralyzed man for one who can walk.

And remember that while poor people may hate rich

people, they hate themselves most of all, for not being rich.

Love money. Don't worship it, and don't be afraid of it, either. But love it.

It's one of those rare loves that actually reaps rewards.

———

Peeetrooos!

Petraaaakis!

Lazaros walks with his eyes trained on the ground and as he moves, they too move over the ground. He walks with his flashlight on, watching his shadow stretch long and thin like a rope tying him to the night he left behind, and to the darkness that awaits him.

As he arrives above Magou Beach, he kneels at the edge of the road and puts his ear to the hard pavement, waiting to hear something. Not something, someone. Not someone, Petros. If he went into the Dragon Cave that night and if the cave stretches, as they say, whole kilometers beneath the island, and if the island is, as they say, hollow in places, then at some point, somehow, he'll hear him. Surely, at some point he'll hear him.

Surely.

Peeetrooos!

Petraaaakis!

Where are you?

His mouth loves his son's name.

He stands up again and lights a cigarette, looking at the dark sea across the way, at the gorge, at Black Cave that gapes like a howling mouth in the face of the rock. That's where Komitis's twins went last year and hanged themselves – first the boy and then his sister, a month later. Twenty years old, what could they know of pain and suffering? And the father's suffering, who thought about that? Poor Komitis. The poor bastard came here without a penny to his name all the way from the other end of Greece, Drama, Xanthi, somewhere up there. At first he opened up a little hole of a shop down at the port and fixed broken cell phones, computers, TVs. Then he patented a GPS app to track sheep and goats and sold it to some Jews and made tons of money. Serious money. And just when he was giving thanks to God and thinking now he could put his feet up for a while, that awful thing befell him – and he was left carrying two coffins on his back for the rest of his life. That poor Komitis. Did anyone bother to consider his pain?

Kids. People raise them these days as if they're the center of the world. They fall all over them the instant they come into the world, cuddle them, kiss them, slobber on them, suck them in as if they're trying to fill some hole inside – mothers, fathers, grandfathers, grandmothers. That's why you see kids growing up as they do, stunted, ugly little runts. Sallow, weak, wimpy, faint-hearted kids, whose parents have been sucking up all their strength and blood since the day they were born – or even earlier, when they were still in the womb. And so they grow up empty, and eventually the time comes for them to have kids of their own and smother them and suck them dry, too, suck out their souls and strength and blood. Family. Soul-sucking vampires. Vampires who give birth to vampires who will give birth to even more vampires when their turn comes. A country of vampires, that's where we're living these days. Vampires.

Lazaros smokes his cigarette, looking at the sea, and remembers again tonight. He remembers how the day after May Day one of Drakakis's goons came to the restaurant, a sissy with tattoos and plucked eyebrows, and asked him where Petros was.

You're asking me? Isn't he with you guys?

Haris sent me, said the sissy. We haven't seen him in days. So we're looking.

How many days?

I don't know. Days.

Did something happen? Was there some kind of fight?

I don't know. Haris sent me to ask.

Petros's cell phone was off. Lazaros tried to get a hold of Drakakis, but he wasn't answering, either. The next morning he brought a case of wine to that drunkard Petihakis, the cop, and had him put out a call to his guys on the other islands. He went to the mayor, the bishop, the hospital director. He went down to the port and talked to all the fishermen and taxi drivers. The most he could unearth, from the gull cop everyone called Listen Up, was that Drakakis came to the island the previous weekend on someone else's yacht and brought a whole crew with him, a dozen or so people.

Was my son with them?

Forget it, chief. No use stirring the fire.

Just tell me, man.

Listen up, just let it go.

Tell me.

OK, well, once the whole lot of them were pretty sloshed that psycho Drakakis came out and grabbed your kid and tied him to the railing and brought over a pair of scissors to cut his hair. Then the other guys came out, too, and a pack of whores who were along for the ride, and, hand to God, they started filling a bunch of condoms with piss and water and chucking them at his head. So humiliating, you couldn't hardly believe it. The poor kid pleaded and shouted, but what's he supposed to do, one guy against that crowd. When they finally let him go, he took off like a shot and jumped into a boat. I hope the devil destroys that asshole Drakakis's family. He and his goons drove that kid mad.

Lazaros listened with his eyes closed.

Are you sure? They saw him getting into the boat?

Listen up, Lazaros, don't get mixed up in this. Those guys are no good.

Where was he headed?

How should I know. Out to sea.

Why didn't you say anything all this time?

For Christ's sake, listen up. You think I know what

you should do with your kid?

The next day he took the fast boat to Piraeus. He went to the company offices, but they wouldn't even let him in the door – they didn't know anything about Petros, and said Drakakis was out of the country and they didn't know when he'd be back. He shouted, he cursed, they practically kicked him out into the street. Petros had told him he was staying temporarily with some friends in Kastela. He didn't have an address, or any idea who the friends might be, so he hiked up there on foot and started wandering through the streets, searching blind, asking people on balconies and in shops if they knew a young guy who looked like this and this, tall, skinny, with black hair down to his shoulders. He was ashamed of how they looked at him, wished the earth would open up and swallow him whole, but he didn't know what else to do. When he got back home, he dropped everything else and spent his days wandering all over the island, from one end to the other. He took the car down every road, from Echo Bay to Pities, from Futility Point to Boatbreak, back and forth, dawn to nightfall, one hand on the wheel, his phone in the other. Petros's cell was dead, Drakakis had vanished,

Petihakis the cop could care less – leave it to me, I've taken action, I'll be in touch. In Tourtouras people said they'd seen a guy who looked like Petros at the old campground, down on the beach, where those stoners from Athens had gathered. He went down and spied on them with binoculars, but didn't see his son. Someone in Hosti had seen a boat abandoned in Fidoussa across the way. He talked Charonis into taking him in his fishing boat, but they didn't find anything. Barbarian Isle, Moray Bay, Murderess, beach by beach they searched all of those tiny, barren islands off the coast, but it was all wasted effort. Some people said they thought they'd seen a boat dragged up onto shore at Galley Slave, others that they'd seen a man crossing Orphan's Stream alone, across the way on Outer Island. He didn't know what to believe, or who to believe. Everyone he asked seemed to have a gleam of cruel joy in their eyes. And then, in Fones, he heard from some rats who worked at the desalinization plant in Meskinia that someone had been hanging around up at the big cave, the Dragon Cave, for the past few days. They'd caught sight of the guy a couple of times as they were coming back on the little ferry from across the way, and they signaled to him with a mirror, just for kicks, but he ran off and hid in the cave.

What did he look like? Lazaros asked. What's he like? Young, old, what?

Must have been young. And tall, skinny.

And his hair? Black, long?

No, real short, like a crew cut.

And you saw him with your own eyes?

You think we saw him with yours?

The very next day he drove to Mougkros and climbed down, rock by rock, all the way to the cave. Outside he saw the remains of a fire, cigarette butts, trash. He went in and shouted, but didn't know how far to keep going – some say the cave stretches all the way to the slopes of Mount War, in the middle of the island, and others say it goes even further, to Outer Island. He went back the next day and the day after that. The fourth day he thought about taking supplies with him – flashlight, food, water – and searching every inch of the cave, no matter how deep it went or how long it took. And he would've, if he weren't afraid Petros might show up in the meantime – and then what would happen? If he went in, Petros was sure to appear.

For sure.

And then what would happen?

Think about it for a minute. No, think about it. Think what would happen if the rats found out you went into the cave to find Petros, and in the meantime Petros showed up and now he has to go into the cave to find you. Just think what a party they'd throw, that's all I'm saying. You'd be the top news item on Rat TV. Who cares about you – but what did the kid do to deserve that kind of ridicule?

They'd even make up folk songs about it.

As sure as I'm seeing you here.

They'd even make up folk songs, those bastards, those snakes.

———◆◆◆———

Lazaros walks with his eyes trained on the ground and as he moves, they, too, move over the ground. He walks and thinks how if this were all a fairy tale, a chilling tale like the ones old people tell on summer nights, a night like tonight, for instance, out in the yard with the grill fired up – because old people still tell tales on this island, only these days they tell them to one another, since there are no more kids to listen, these days kids want to be scared by other things, and that's progress, that's freedom, that's equality and democracy, to be free even as a child to choose what kind of fear suits you best – if it were all nothing but a story full of goblins and liver-eating vampires, billy goats that laugh and speak with human tongues, soldiers' ghosts crying out and fires that flare up and die down all on their own on the first nights of August, across from Slave Isle – if this were all a fairytale, he'd be carrying white pebbles in his pockets to toss behind him so he could find his way back out, if it were a fairy tale, if all this were a fairy tale, if only it were a fairy tale.

Because fairy tales have happy endings. Fairy tales always end well. Right? Right. They lived well and we live even better. Of course. That's how the story goes.

Lazaros is using his flashlight now that the moon has disappeared and as he walks he says, imagine, the way things are headed, soon enough anyone who goes out in search of a lost child will have a sponsor, you can quote me on that, and I wish that's how it was already, I wish I had on a red Vodafone cap, or a shirt from Cosmote or Jumbo, I wish I had a sponsor to bring out a crowd and turn the whole island upside down, and pay for fishing boats and helicopters that would search for Petros day and night, because then we'd find him for sure, if I had a sponsor backing me we'd probably have found him already.

What can one father do on his own?

How many caves can he enter, how many gorges can he climb down, how many deserted beaches can he comb?

Lazaros mutters to himself as he walks, louder and louder, trying to trick himself into thinking he isn't alone, to trick the darkness into thinking he isn't alone, because the truth is he's scared tonight, it's the first time he's done the rounds of the island on foot – at first he took the truck, but that didn't seem like the best way to get the job done – and now he's even more afraid because he sees the chapel of Christ our Lord glistening white before him, the one with the old well beside it where they say the island's sprites hide, babies who died before they were baptized, with sharp teeth and curly hair, black wings, flushed cheeks, and nails as long and yellow as a blackbird's beak.

As he arrives outside the chapel, he stands and pulls the flask of tsikoudia out of his vest pocket and takes a long swig, to wash down the fear. Then he kneels and pulls his black-handled knife – which, as everyone knows, can ward off evil things – out of its sheath and uses it to trace a circle in the soil around his feet. He pulls out the pistol with his left hand and, kneeling there inside the circle, holding the knife in one hand and the pistol in the other, he leans back, takes a deep breath, and with his eyes closed raises his head to a sky punctured by a thousand stars.

Peeetroooos!

Petraaaakis!

Dooo youououou heeeaaaar meee?

He shouts again and again, with all the strength in his body, drawing out the *ouououou* like a wolf, feeling a shiver climbing up from his legs to his heart, praying that when he stops howling he'll hear not the screeches of sprites but the voice of his son, praying for Christ our Lord to bring him a miracle, tonight, or tomorrow, praying for an end to this agony, praying to see his son again, to clutch his son's body to his own, to stroke that long hair, those unshaven cheeks, the soft fuzz on his spine.

Peeetrooos!

Peeetrooos!

With his eyes shut he holds his breath, hoping to hear something. Nothing. Even the sprites are quiet tonight. He falls to the ground and presses his ear to the soil. He waits. He counts to fifty and then to a hundred, and as he counts, all he hears is a voice inside him saying the same words again and again, like a riddle.

If you lose your father they call you an orphan.
If you lose your wife they call you a widower.
If you lose your child, what do they call you?
What do they call you?
What?

———◊◊◊———

What do they call you if you lose your child, what do they call you, what do they call you, what, what, what do they call you, what, Lazaros the Bow mutters to himself as he walks – Lazaros, Lazaros, as bent as a bow yourself, you poor, abandoned creature – and as he passes over the rushing stream of Kardiokaftis he sees a tiny light flickering on the other side and for an instant his chest swells, Petros, Petrakis, and he starts to raise the flashlight into the air, Petros, Petrakis, but

then his hand falls again like a dry leaf, it's only Perou-
lakis, the cop, who's out there again tonight guarding
the fields of that mafioso Varipatis, a cop by day who
guards watermelons at night, at least in summer, in
winter he guards oranges, three hundred a month all
year round, what am I supposed to do, with the mess
those traitor politicians landed us in, three hundred is
nothing to sneeze at, three hundred pays for milk and
diapers, though it's tough staying up all night like a
vampire, tough pretending that night is just another day,
but I'd rather guard melons than hash, if you know what
I mean, there's a lot of bad shit going on down here, you
might not see it, Lazaros, because you're a measured
man, a family man, God bless, but there are plenty of
guys over in Little Athens who are worse than Albanians,
give them an eye and they'll ask for the eyebrow, too,
and sure, I don't like how they call you guys foreigners
either, but you get what I'm saying, and of course those
bastard mongrels down at the campground get up to
stuff you wouldn't believe, how did this country get so
rough, man, I mean, on the nights when I sit up here all
alone I think about all kinds of things, I say to myself,
how did we end up like this, how did we sour on one

another so much, how can it be that on a tiny island like this we can't live together, just a drop of a place and we're at one another's throats, you call us rats and we call you foreigners, and then I wonder if we were always like this, if the fact that we could cheat one another, steal from one another is what kept us together all these years, if it was the lying and cheating and fake money, if that's the only reason we put up with one another, that's the sort of stuff I think about when I sit here late into the night and my soul hurts, because I don't know what's worse, to love your country because you're ripping it off or to hate it because you can't do that anymore, and I think how now that the money is gone we have to find something else to keep us together, but I can't think of what, I can't see that there's anything left, there's just nothing, nothing, nothing – Lazaros moves forward with the flashlight switched off in his hand, which hangs at his side as dry as a carob pod, and his head echoes with the words of Peroulakis who guards melons and oranges for three hundred a month, and he increases his speed, trying to put that place behind him faster, so Perou-lakis won't see him and call him over and start in on the same crybaby routine, empty words, cheap words, a welter of empty talk, a whole load of their cheaplish, as Charonis calls it – because words matter, of course, but what matters more is who's speaking – and with the flashlight switched off Lazaros walks and thinks again of all the people he's run into on these nights when he drags himself from one side of the island to the other, Peroulakis who guards Varipatis's fields, Chryssi who wanders barefoot over the deserted beaches and talks to the stars, Gouigouis whose grandkids kicked him out of his house so they could turn it into a bed and breakfast, Comeandgo, Asimoyiannis, old lady Pandora, Sifounios who rides his horse in red cowboy boots – people like ghosts, or ghosts like people, ghosts who are more afraid of people than people are of ghosts.

When he comes to the forest of Nohia, he turns the flashlight on again and looks from a distance at the solid pines the north wind has bent, their trunks hanging just a half meter above the ground, and from far off they look like warriors who've been shot right in the chest, only instead of falling in a heap to the ground, they stayed suspended in the air with their arms spread wide, as if condemned to remain there for all eternity, frozen, hanging in the air, neither upright nor fallen –

and then he starts walking again and enters the forest, looking up at the trees, going deeper into the forest, and as he points his hand here and there the light from the flashlight looks to him like a bird that woke startled by the light, and is fluttering between dark branches, looking for a way out, trying to fly far off, to escape, but it's all a lie, a lie, a lie, because now the forest looks like Salamander's head after he got fired and all his hair fell out in a single night, even his eyebrows and lashes, that's what the forest looks like now, Salamander's head, plucked bare, with a few scattered trees here and there, pine trees, arbutus, oaks and holly oaks – they ruined the place again this winter, turning the trees into logs for fireplaces and wood stoves. Lazaros moves through the devastated forest and wishes he could hear all the old sounds, the yellowhammer's complaining cheep cheep, the harsh chik chik of the .wren, the tiou tiou of the corn bunting, the crazy trills of the crested lark, the turtledove's tur tur tur, and above all, above all, the blackbird's sweet call – if consolation had a voice, it would be a blackbird's voice beyond all doubt – Lazaros goes deeper into the forest, looking up, eyes and ears wide open, but he hears nothing at all, only the leaves crunching like gristle beneath his boots, his own wheezing breath, the beating of his heart.

And when he comes out the other side, where the ascent for Second Coming begins, he turns right and goes and stands at the edge of the gorge and looks at the lake spreading before him. He looks silently at the black water that glows as if it's swallowed a bit of light from the moon, at the reeds that echo with the croaking of frogs, at the mud that looks reddish in the dark, as if the soil has been kneaded with blood.

Peeetrooos!

Petraaakiiis!

Lazaros, eyes closed, shouts into this wasteland, again and again, shouts until the twin dogs of worry and fear begin once more to nip mercilessly at his chest, shouts until his lungs give way, shouts knowing that the cruel north wind will take his voice, toy with it for a while, and then break its neck, suffocate it slowly, sweetly, sleepily.

But Lazaros keeps shouting – that's how much his mouth loves the name of his son.

Peeetrooos!

Petraaaakis!

– 175 –

And then, exhausted, coughing and wheezing like an old asthmatic dog, he drops to his knees and puts his ear to the hard earth, eyes closed, and waits to hear something. Not something, someone. Not someone, Petros. If he went into the Dragon Cave that night, and if the cave stretches, as they say, whole kilometers beneath the island, and if the island is, as they say, hollow in places, then at some point, he'll surely be able to hear him. If, if, if, sounds like a lot of ifs, you'll say. And I'll answer you right back that ifs like that are what made humans human, that ifs are still what makes the world turn. If you believe only what you hear, there's no way you'll hear the things you believe. And then you'll ask, what do I, a taverna owner, know about any of that, come on, Lazaros, you'll say, enough with the folk wisdom, go and grab us a cold beer, and I'll say that if the deaf weren't too deaf to hear the guy telling them they're deaf, there would be fewer deaf people in the world. Now take a swig of that beer.

Where's your smartaleck stuff now?

That shut you up, huh?

Since you're deaf, how are you supposed to speak?

All ifs are good, there's just one that scares me.

If you lose your father they call you an orphan. If you lose your wife they call you a widower. If you lose your child, what do they call you?

That's the only if I'm afraid of.

If you lose your child, what do they call you?

If.

What?

—❧—

It's almost four. Just two hours until daybreak. From Murderer's Gorge Lazaros sees the "Arkadi" puffing off toward Piraeus, but doesn't stop to look. He still has a long way to go and needs to get there in time, by six he needs to be up above the Dragon Cave, so he can see the sun rise, because there's no doubt about it, it's a beautiful thing to see the sun rise, it's a good sign to see a new day dawn, the light of the sun brings hope, no matter how much darkness you have inside, the light of the sun is a kind of hope, and besides, as that dimwit Charonis said the other day, we should believe in the sun not only because we see it, but because it's what lets us see everything else.

Lazaros is limping now as he walks, with obstinate

steps and eyes trained on the ground, and as he moves they too move over the ground. His boots are covered in red mud and he doesn't want to look at them because it's as if tonight he's once again passed through fields soaked in blood. Lazaros limps as he walks, to get there in time to see the sun rising out of the sea, and hears something inside him saying that the day that's about to begin will be a red-letter day, something will happen today, you'll see, today you'll see good coming from the sea, today you'll see Petros again and when you do you'll rush at him, run toward him, grab him in your arms, you'll squeeze and squeeze until you hear him say, Dad, stop, you're hurting me, Dad, but you still won't listen, you'll just squeeze and kiss, smell and caress, the unshaven cheeks, that long hair, the fuzz on his spine, that's how it'll be, Lazaros limps forward, trying to forget the exhaustion and pain, he's tired, worn out from walking all those hours, his boots are leaden, his feet are so swollen it feels like he has four of them, two in each boot, and he keeps breaking into a sweat, then getting cold again, and all the things he's carrying feel like dead weight, he'd like to throw it all off, if only he had the balls to get rid of his clothes, his pistols and knives, and unarmed, naked, newly unburdened, he'd be so light he could run as if he were eighteen again, run like Petros, hey, folks, come and see, loonybin Lazaros stripped down to his birthday suit and lost his shit with the refubees, come and see, all the devils jumped into him and never came back out again.

Lazaros limps, out of breath, limps forward full of regret, because he's decided he was wrong to believe what the guys in Fones said about the Dragon Cave, they must've been lying, those sons of bitches tricked him and now they're sitting somewhere and laughing at him – Petros never hid in any cave, his son isn't a rat, he wouldn't sneak off to hide in holes and caves, that's not how he raised his boy. He must've taken the boat to some deserted island, some out-of-the-way place, and decided to stay there long enough to clear his mind, think things over, collect himself. That's what happened, for sure. You might ask, what does he do all day out there in the middle of nowhere, and for so many days? What does he eat, where does he sleep, where does he find water? And I'll answer right back that you don't know shit, you can't even put two and two together, you're like these fools down here, with a fly's brain and the heart of a snake. Did you really believe Listen Up's fairy tales, the stories that rat pawned off on you? Did you really believe that Petros, my Petros, two meters tall and as strong as an ox, would sit and let that squirt Drakakis cut his hair and humiliate him in front of everyone? They lied to you, don't you see? It happened the other way around. He must've gotten all bent out of shape at seeing someone else get treated that way and chased the bastards down and kicked them all to kingdom come, then took the boat and went and found a place where he could be alone, to calm down, to drain all that hatred from his soul. What does he eat and drink, you ask. I'll tell you what he eats and drinks. He eats fish he catches himself and drinks the water he brought with him on the boat. And he sleeps like a baby, like a little bird in the boat, the waves rocking him to sleep. Remember what we used to sing in the navy?

> *I am the sailor*
> *of the Aegean*
> *my bed is the waves*
> *and my heart pumps fire*
> *for our glorious land*

I'll brave the creatures
of the wide, dark sea
and the winds and storms
and await eagerly
the time to come
when boldly we'll fight
our hated enemy.

He closes his eyes for a moment and tries to imagine how it'll be. How it'll be to see Petros coming from the sea. He'll come from the sea, that's the only thing that's certain. Good will come from the sea. Unshaven, his hair a mess, his eyes red from heartache, the salt breeze, and lack of sleep. And Lazaros won't say a thing. Nothing, nothing at all. He'll just take him in his arms and squeeze him tight, smell him and kiss him, countless kisses, he'll pinch his cheeks, stroke his long hair, kiss him again and again on the mouth, the cheeks, the eyes. That's how it'll be. Petros will come from the sea. For sure. That's the only sure thing. It's the only way. That's where he'll come from, for sure.

Good will come from the sea.

Lazaros limps forward as fast as he can, but his tongue moves faster than his feet, calling out marching songs, curses, prayers, spinning like a wheel – it's all lies, you hear me, lies, he wouldn't let them touch a hair on his head, I raised the boy so I should know, he won't let anyone tell him what to do, he probably beat them all like drums and then took the boat and went off to some deserted beach to calm down, to clear his mind, that's what happened, Lazaros limps forward as fast as he can, so he'll get to the Dragon Cave in time to see the sun coming out big and strong and red, it's all lies, and if you really want to know I don't care what they call someone who loses his child, I couldn't care less, I'm a widower and an orphan, sure, but I'm not that other thing, what-ever they call it, I'm not that, I haven't lost my child, it was just a scare, I got shaken up, but it'll pass, maybe even today, because I know everything's fine, every-thing's fine, he's just a kid, a man, he does crazy things sometimes, you think we weren't as bad when we were young, everything's fine, I'm telling you, it's all fine, it was a dream and now it's over, like when you see a dead fish in your dream and you worry it's a bad omen, but now everything's fine, tutto bene, everything's bien, everything's a-okay, let's all make hay, and just you wait till my Petrakis comes back, we'll have the biggest party you've ever seen, and the rats will pass by outside and stare at us, mouths hanging open, what are you looking at, bastards, what are you looking at, bitches, come over if you dare, come on over, we've got condoms, too, only ours aren't full of water. Step right up, come on in. Petros, son, go get the cock socks. The boys came over for target practice.

Come on in, bastards. Come on in, bitches.

At the crossroads, between Beast's Hole and Mougkros, he stops and bends over to catch his breath. By now his legs are as heavy as an elephant's, sweat drips down into his eyes, hot, bitter, yellow, gallons of tsikoudia, tons of nicotine. Just a little bit longer. An hour more. Then he'll rest once and for all. Courage. It's not much farther. Courage.

It'll be dawn in an hour.

———

If you're looking down from the peak of the rock, two

hundred fathoms above the sea, the cave is hidden from view. You have to take the overgrown path down to the middle of the slope, pass through the dark gorge, and then, when you emerge on the other side, climb down another twenty fathoms until you reach the mouth of the cave, which gapes pitch black between sharp boulders. And it has to be a calm day for you to manage all that, because the face of the rock is exposed to the wind, and when it blows at full strength, it doesn't leave a stone standing up there.

Lazaros has been in the cave three times in the past few days, and each time he spat blood to get down there, and to get back up afterward. Dizzy, scared, hands chafed raw, at times he thought he would surely leave his bones there on the rocks. And yet he would climb down again today if there were any reason to. But there isn't. It's over, it's all cleared up, no sense talking about it anymore. Petros will come from the sea, not the cave. That's how it'll happen, for sure.

I know it.

He glances over the black cliff that yawns beneath his feet, then steps back and sits and takes off his boots and socks. He loosens the sheath of his hunting knife from his calf, pulls the pistol out of his belt, strips off his vest and shirt. He sets it all by his side, along with the walking stick and flashlight, and stretches his bruised and swollen legs. He lies down on his back on the damp rock, feeling a sweet shiver spread through his limbs. Then he lifts his legs in the air and with a single sudden movement pulls off his pants and underwear together. Naked now, he splays his arms and legs wide and with his eyes closed lets his body cool, rest, breathe. He smiles at the thought that when Petros arrives in the boat he'll see a little man off in the distance, entirely naked, jumping up and down and waving his arms on the peak of the rock.

The day will be dawning any moment now. He can tell from how the north wind is slowly gathering strength, rippling the sea, and carrying the scents of oregano, sage, and rosemary all the way up to where he is – scents that make Lazaros's nostrils quiver and his heart beat more quickly because they remind him of other times, heroic times, times when he felt sure and strong, sure he would become somebody, not nobody, a whole man, not half a man, a man who wouldn't know how it feels to say I'm afraid or I can't, a man who struggled to bring life to his size rather than let life cut him down to its size instead. A whole man, not half a man.

We're fine, says Lazaros, looking at the dim light that's starting to glow off in the distance, behind the white clouds. It was just a scare, it'll pass. And if we said hurtful things to one another, it's fine, we're men. I did it for you. So you wouldn't end up like those little people who waste their lives grazing on nickels and dimes because they don't have the balls to get out there and hunt down the real money. And if you're going to hunt for money you have to go out with the guys who know how to hunt. I did it for you, hear? So you wouldn't live a life full of hate. That's why poor people suffer. First they hate people with money, then they hate themselves for being poor, and finally they end up hating the whole world. And hatred is the worst thing of all, even worse than money. That's why I told you, my boy, that you have to learn to love money. So your heart doesn't fill with hate. I did it for you. Do you hear me, Petrakis? My light, my life, do you hear me?

He gets to his feet and looks again over the edge of the cliff, measuring the darkness between him and the darkness down there. His knees buckle, he feels something tremble inside him, low, between his legs. He takes a step back and kneels on the rock and decides to await the new day just like that, naked, on his knees.

I may have been wrong, though. Do you hear me, Petrakis? Petros, Petrakis, my good boy. You hear what I'm saying? I may have been wrong. There may be some other way, some other path. Maybe you'll find that other path and follow it. Maybe you already did. Come back, my boy, come back and do as you like. I swear I won't ever tell you what to do again. Come and say I'm a crazy old fool, a drunk, nothing but a taverna owner. Come and say whatever you like, curse me up and down, tell me I'm a piece of trash. But come back. Let me see you again, my Petros, that's all I want. When you're here, two hearts beat in my chest. Without you, there's none at all. Petros, Petrakis, my good boy. Come back to me. Come, my light. My Petros. Come.

On his knees, Lazaros pleads, mutters to himself, eyes wide-open, hands hugging his arms, until his voice becomes a whisper and finally disappears, it too blown away on the north wind which is still gathering strength.

Day breaks, and Lazaros the Bow, naked, kneeling, silent, stares with wide-open eyes at the sun as it rises from the horizon like a burning fingertip a baby giant is raising ever so timidly into the sky, a baby from some other world lifting its finger to touch for the first time, mad with anticipation and joy, the clouds to the east that keep swapping color for color, turning white and silver and yellow, then orange and red, deep red clouds, huge clouds that seem born not of water but of an endless sea of blood.

On July 9, 1956, our island was hit by the biggest tsunami the Aegean ever saw. My father says he remembers that day clearly – though in 1956 he hadn't even been born. The earthquake happened at five in the morning, 7.5 on the Richter scale, south of Amorgos, and an hour later, the tsunami broke at a speed of three hundred kilometers an hour against Inner Island and destroyed everything in its path, from up above the Dragon Cave all the way down to Boatbreak. At Hosti the waves reached a height of 25 meters and broke a whole kilometer inland, all the way to the Hanged Man's stream. Fishing boats, houses, fields, all gone. For three whole days the color of the sea turned from blue to red and gray. And the people, who were still living in the dark ages and had no idea what a tsunami was, or underwater erosion and shallow depths of focus, climbed up to the top of Mount War and hid in caves and dropped to their knees and begged forgiveness from God, because they were certain that the Second Coming was at hand.

As if it were yesterday, my father says. I remember it all. There were signs back then, and signs now, too. Lots of signs back then, and even more now. If you see a big fire burning by the sea and people rifling through the charred remains, you can be sure the end is coming. And if you see a turtle with a long nail stuck clean through its head, coming back out at the base of its neck, and it doesn't die all at once but slowly and torturously of starvation, you can be sure the end is coming. Unless. Unless, he says, smiling, and winks at me. You understand.

Of course, I say. I understand you perfectly. Loud and clear. Loud and clear, over and out. All the way out, as out as it gets.

Bravo, that's my girl. Come over here and I'll kiss you a clover, one, two, three kisses make a clover – and a fourth makes it lucky. You got that, too, right? Smart as a jackal, my girl.

Have you ever been kissed by someone who's had a stroke? Isn't it strange? The twisted mouth, the frothy saliva, the breath that smells of pills and something burnt. The mouth, that's the hardest part. It's a true art to manage to be suitably kissed by a crooked mouth, to stand properly

– 190 –

before a crooked mouth that wants to kiss you more than anything.

That night his shouts woke me. He was sitting up in bed, holding a long nail in his good hand, his left. I froze. I said to myself, now he's going to swallow it or plunge it into one of his eyes and that'll be that, it'll all be over. Where did he find that nail, can you tell me that? I'm asking, I'm really asking. He can't even get out of bed on his own. Where did he find it? He gestured to me with his hand to come closer. In the dim light he seemed so pale and thin, as if he were already gone.

It's fine, we saved it, he said. Fortunately the brain wasn't harmed. I put on some waterproof antiseptic. It's still pretty dazed, but I think it'll pull through. But there's a lot of pain there, a lot of suffering. At any rate, I'm optimistic. It'll pull through.

He raised the nail above his head and looked at it, then placed it in my palm and closed his fingers around mine.

Keep this, he said, to remember me by. Remember how I fought until the very end, fought to keep the end at bay. Remember that.

Kites in July

What makes rainbows curved?

Artemis raised her arm and with one outstretched finger traced the arc of the rainbow that seemed to stretch all the way from Naxos to Amorgos and beyond. It had stopped raining only a short while ago, and the sea still churned and the sky to the west was already starting to darken again.

Why are they curved? she asked once more.

Come on, let's get out of here, Stavros said. Looks to me like we're headed for more rain.

He stood and tried to shake the dark specks off his legs. The air smelled burnt. He could barely believe it. Two days later and the burnt smell was still there. Those rats had done a fine job. Real professionals. It was all ash now, nothing was left standing. Only the walls, but when the real rains came in winter they would fall too. After all, this had just been a summer shower and it still dragged the rubble all the way to the sea. It scattered charred objects everywhere, and the water ran black between the rocks. The air smelled burnt, too. He could barely believe it.

He could barely believe any of it.

He glanced over at Artemis who was sitting on a rock, still running her finger between the rainbow's two ends. He thought about telling her it was bad luck to point at a rainbow but knew how she would respond, so he kept quiet. She'd set a few bottles of wine by her feet that for some reason hadn't burst in the fire. She found some other things, too, digging through the ruins. New things, old things, things they bought specifically for the restaurant and others they'd brought with them from Athens. The painting they had hung near the door, of a tall, lean sprite dressed in bright colors, like the joker in a deck of cards, skipping along playing a pipe with a pack of rats trailing behind. A windmill with blades like white birds, a bronze mermaid sitting on a rock, two lanterns shaped like lighthouses, and a small orange life preserver that said mermaids welcome on it in white letters. Those were the sorts of things she had picked out of the ruins. Their things, blackened, distorted.

Are you ready? he said. Let's go.

He climbed down to the sea, rock by rock, washed his hands, then stood and looked up at the rainbow, too. It truly was huge. He closed first his right eye and then the left because he'd heard somewhere that rainbows look different if you look at them through different eyes.

It looked exactly the same to him.

When he came back up to where Artemis was sitting, she'd lit a cigarette and was staring cross-eyed at the smoke rising white and thick from her mouth. She had black specks all over, on her cheeks, her arms, her legs, her ankles. Her shirt, skirt, and sandals were blackened with ash. She looked like a miner.

Get up, let's go.

No. Go home and get the kite.

Get up already, I said.

No. I want the kite.

They looked at one another like cats.

Please, do me that favor, Artemis said. Will you do that for me? Don't you love me anymore?

His eyes stung. He rubbed them with his thumbs and they stung even more. A breeze had picked up and Artemis's hair was blowing around like a torn flag. She pushed it out of her eyes with one hand, smearing black

fingerprints over her forehead. She looked like a miner.
A miner or an Indian covered in war paint.

As he headed for the car, he heard her calling to
him. She was holding a bottle of wine by its neck and
waving it in the air.

Bring something to open this, too, she shouted. I
want us to get wasted tonight.

———— ∞ ————

They used to dream. Staring out at the sea. That's
why they decided to call the place Good Will Come
From the Sea. It wasn't going to be just your regular
ouzeri. It wouldn't even be an ouzeri. They weren't sure
what it would be, only that it would be something
different, something unique. They dreamed all kinds of
dreams, had all sorts of ideas. They knew their dreams
were bigger than what they could actually accomplish,
but they couldn't stop. They dreamed of doing things
not just for themselves but for others, too. They couldn't
change the world, but they could at least change a small
piece of it.

You know what we are? Artemis asked Stavros.
We're the planet by its proper name. Remember how

you once told me that so much of the globe is covered in water that we should really call it Water, not Earth? That's what we are. The planet by its proper name. And we're like that fairy tale, too, about the village that was overrun by rats and one day a guy in brightly colored clothes with a magic pipe started playing and charmed the rats and they followed him into the sea and drowned. That's what we are.

They used their compensation money on the renovations. It was an old fish taverna, on the water, between Agiathalassa and Paradeisia. Artemis's uncle, the German, had bought it years earlier for the land, planning to knock it down and build a summer home there. But then his wife, an Italian woman with two kids from her first marriage, made him buy a villa in Sardinia, in a place called Costa Smeralda, where Berlusconi and Niarchos apparently had villas, too, and a scoop of ice cream cost twenty euros, so the taverna sat there, abandoned, worn away by the weather and the salt from the sea. Last winter, when they'd decided to move to the island, Artemis called her uncle in Germany. He was pleased at her news and told her to take the keys and go and stay in the taverna for as long as they liked. But they didn't need a place to live. They'd found one, small and cheap, in Little Athens. They were looking for a business. Her uncle needed some time to think it over. He was a methodical man, had his systems in place, and never made hasty decisions.

Give me a few days to talk it over with Aunt Mauretta, he told Artemis.

He was the president of a pharmaceutical company. He had Greek blood, a German mind, and an Italian wife. He went skiing in the Alps, had a huge villa in Sardinia, traveled for work to Beijing, London, New York. He was a true cosmopolitan.

A week later they talked on Skype to settle the details. A two-year contract, five hundred a month, no deposit. They would start paying rent in September. The first three months, the whole summer, was on him, for good luck.

Artemis was thrilled. But Stavros didn't like it one bit. He didn't like her uncle, either, saw him as one of those guys who went from Raphael to Gaphael without looking back, Greeks who ended up even more German than the Germans. Just listening to him talk turned Stavros's stomach.

Allo, Stavgos. It's uncle Gaphael calling from Stuttgart.

They would talk for a minute, then Stavros would call Artemis to the phone.

Achtemis, come heag, please. It's your uncle Gaphael from Stuttgagt.

Artemis would come running, biting her lip, and pinch him to make him stop.

He didn't like Raphael one bit. More German than a German. You folks down there, he'd say to Stavros. You folks down there do this, do that. You folks down there need to learn to work. To stop crying over spilled milk and figure out how to stand on your own two feet. No one owes you anything. You know what's to blame? Your backwards ways. Two hundred years later, you still haven't decided if you want to be European. I mean, who do you think you are? Really, who?

He had a whole theory. According to him, over the past few years, Greece had committed the perfect crime. Actual perpetrators: politicians. Moral perpetrators: voters. Motive: to buy people's conscience. Weapon: money – foreign money, black market money, easy money. Victim: the nation.

That was his theory in a nutshell. And as much as Stavros felt like giving him a piece of his mind in return, he always held his tongue.

Do us a favor and go fuck yourself, uncle Raphael, he wanted to say. Everyone's always pointing fingers at this crime or that, but the Germans sure are ones to speak. And drop that line about Europe already. What Europe? Europe only ever existed on maps and in books. And don't start in on Plato and Aristotle and the Romans. We're talking about now, and about normal people. What do I have to do with a Dane, a Swede, a Czech? And what exactly was our crime? The fact that we wanted a shingle or two over our heads, wanted to buy a car? I mean, what were we supposed to do? Live in caves and ride around on mules? You'll be sending us back there before you know it. To an era of caves and mules. And as for caves, fine. But who knows where we'll even find mules to ride, by that point we'll probably have eaten them all.

That's how he wanted to respond. But he didn't say anything. So Artemis had to bear the brunt of it.

Just imagine, us living in the taverna. What does he take us for, Pakistanis or something? And can I say one more thing? If I had his millions I would help as many people as I could. I wouldn't sit there and charge my own niece five hundred a month for that ruin. The cheapskate. What's the use of relatives like that? Instead of him saying, sure, take the place, it's yours, and here's thirty thousand to get things off on the right foot – instead of him telling you that, he has the gumption to ask for rent and contracts and all the rest. That cheapskate has no shame. What an asshole.

Are you insane? Artemis said. Instead of thanking the heavens that we found a place that's ready to go, on the very best stretch of waterfront, you have the nerve to talk about him like that? Where else would you ever find a place like that for that kind of money? They'd want two or three thousand, at the very least. The guy's doing us a favor. And he needs the rent for tax purposes.

Yeah, big favor, Stavros said. He should've just given you the deed. That would've been a favor.

Stavros.

What? Am I wrong?

Pull yourself together, please. And stop complaining. Don't expect favors from anyone. Whatever we do, we'll do it ourselves. That's how things work. Got it?

Jawohl, fgau Artemis. Stavgos understand.

Get it together, I'm telling you. We're foreigners here.

What do you mean, foreigners? Fuck that shit. Foreigners? Where do you think we are? Canada? Australia? Is it still fucking Greece here or is it not?

What matters isn't where you are but how you are, Artemis replied. If you're in need, if you're on the outside, you're a foreigner everywhere.

Stavros stubbed out his cigarette and put on his coat.

Where are you going?

I can't stand to listen to you talk like him. I'm going to get some air. It stinks of Germans in here.

They started to get the place ready in January, after the holidays. Bit by bit, week by week, thousand by thousand. Plumbers, refrigerator repairmen, electricians. Whitewashers, painters, floor guys – every dog in the pack. They spent their days haggling and their evenings dreaming. All kinds of dreams, crazy dreams, dreams by the sea. Good will come from the sea. Stavros said it was bad luck for them to dream so much, but he couldn't stop himself, either. The first year would be tough, for sure. Real tough. And the second year, too. But after that, things would start to find a rhythm. They would set a little money aside and plow the rest back into the place. Later, they would buy the restaurant and the plot of land and would get the German off their backs for good. They would plant a vegetable garden and an orchard, everything organic, so they wouldn't have to depend on rats who tried to pass off Chinese garlic and Dutch tomatoes as local produce. Next they'd buy a boat and Stavros would go out fishing, so they wouldn't have to buy fish from rats who pumped them full of chemicals, like mummies. Then they'd buy olive trees to make their own oil, and grapes to make wine and tsikoudia. After that, they'd buy a big stretch of land up in Agrimia where they could raise their own livestock. They would make yogurt and cheese, their own eggs, their own milk. They'd make everything themselves, and have no need of any rats at all.

Everything would be theirs.

So they wouldn't need the rats at all, on land or on sea.

They had other plans, too. They would build an eco-friendly hotel where they would use only local products – no more Luprak, Lipton, or Amita. Then they'd open a store where they'd sell local things, too, and eventually build an entire network for the production and distribution of local goods. And whatever money they made, they would keep on the island, to help others start new businesses and heal the wounds the rats had inflicted on this place over the years, building whatever they pleased, wherever they pleased, however they pleased, stealing from one another and collectively robbing everyone else, working three months out of the year and spending the other nine vacationing in the Seychelles or Gstaad, charging five euros for an espresso and ten for a Greek salad, importing frozen roosters in March and pawning them off as fresh and local in August, serving crocodile in Abyssalos and bison in Rigos, taking money from European Union programs to build bed and breakfasts and using it to dig foundations in the middle of nowhere, which they abandoned without access roads, or electricity, or water, pretending their arid, rocky land was fields so as to cash in on farming subsidies, hiring thugs to strongarm people and smash shop windows, smuggling in whole shiploads of knock-off liquor from the parallel economy, and generally greasing the palms of every mayor, tax officer, and cop around.

They had so many plans, so many dreams. And when they sat arm in arm on the rocks and gazed out at the sea, Artemis would remember the last Christmas they'd spent in Athens, before they left for the island, when they went out to shop for presents and everyone was so polite in all the stores, wished them a merry Christmas and a happy New Year, and looked at them so expectantly, with an expression in their eyes that wasn't grasping or greedy, just full of melancholy and longing, and she remembered telling Stavros how badly she wished they had money, lots of money, so they could go into all the shops and buy something from each place, and remembered telling him for the thousandth time how ever since she was a little girl she'd wanted to give, to give something to everyone, for no particular reason – because what's the use of living if you can't give, and if you can't give to everyone, at least give to those around you, give without expecting anything in return, give without taking anything in exchange, always be the one to take the first step and, yes, I know stuff like this is in fashion these days, everyone says it, and I know that the best way to destroy something good isn't to fight it but to mock it, degrade it, turn it into an internet meme, an electoral slogan, an announcement on TV, but I really believe it, I believe it more than anything, and I know it's not terribly original, it's nothing earth-shattering, I know it's all been said a thousand times, but that may be true of everything in life that really matters, and anyhow, just because something isn't original doesn't mean it isn't true, in fact maybe that's how the truth usually is – monotonous, boring, not original at all.

That's one hell of a head you've got on your shoulders, Stavros said. It'll make us millionaires one day.

They dreamed all night, every night. Even when they came home exhausted from work – Artemis from the souvlaki stand, Stavros from his delivery route with the truck – they would go out onto the rocks and stare for hours at the water, at the stars, the clouds skidding across the sky, the lights from other islands, the lights on ships passing by on the open sea, the lights on fishing boats casting out nets, or pulling them up again, so many lights flickering in the darkness. They would sit side by side smoking or drinking wine, would talk or listen silently to the plash of the waves, and Stavros would bury his face in her hair, trying to catch a whiff of bitter almond beneath the smell of grilled meat, trying to forget the days when her hair smelled only of bitter almond and never of grilled meat, trying to forget, trying to learn to forget, to forget, to forget.

They dreamed of fixing up the restaurant, later, once they had found their footing, to look like a boat, with masts and sails, a prow and a stern, a bridge, even a hold. They'd given it a lot of thought, and it seemed like a great idea.

An ark for the good that would come from the sea.

It was a great idea, really.

And useful, too, for the end of the world.

⸺

He left the car down at the square, behind the church of Saint Marina, and ran up the hill to the house so the neighbors wouldn't catch sight of him and start in again on their condolences and questions. What a terrible thing, Stavros, one guy would say, and another would ask, have the police found anything? Of course they had. Sure, all kinds of stuff, hairs, fingerprints, traces of sperm – they've got it all. Any minute now Horatio Caine is going to jet in from Miami to take a look at the evidence. We're on the right path. It's just a matter of time, they'll probably have the whole investigation wrapped up in a few days. The perpetrators will be arrested and brought to justice. The festering wound will burst. The scalpel will dig deep and clean out the wound. The bratwurst will tickle the throat. Oh, sorry, that's from a different show.

He ducked into the house, went to the window, and looked out from behind the curtain, turning his head to one side like a bird reflected in the side mirror of a car. He was out of breath and as soon as he lit a cigarette he started coughing so hard he almost choked. His breath seemed tinged with the taste of blood. He looked out again through the curtain. It had been her idea to find a place in Little Athens. He wanted them to live outside of town, in one of the nearby villages. He knew what would happen. He knew sooner or later everyone would start treating the place like their own, coming and going whenever they liked. This isn't a neighborhood, it's a commune. And what's with the name, half the people here aren't even from Athens. They barge into their neighbor's house whenever they please, drop off sugar, borrow coffee, bring spanakopita, take a bottle of wine, eat together, drink together, stay up together until all hours. That's the worst, those late nights. Talking for hours, straight through until dawn. Everyone wants to tell you their story, and it's all shit that happened a year or two ago, but the way they talk, you'd think they were unwinding yarns from the war or even before. Once, they say. Once, years ago – and then they tell you about something that happened in 2007 or 2008 or even 2010. What a bunch of kooks. They all sit around pouring out their pain, hanging their dirty laundry out to dry. They laugh, sometimes they cry, even laugh and cry at the same time. Sometimes they're talking about layoffs, bankruptcies and evictions, and the next minute they switch to parties, trips, vacations. Men talk about their wives, women about their husbands, fathers about their sons, mothers about their daughters. They talk about old folks and children, grandfathers and grandmothers, nieces and nephews and grandkids, the living and the dead. Everyone talks, all the time, and all at once.

Hey, buddy, Stavros would nudge Stathis, who was a security guard at the nuthouse in Rigos. Can't you take them all over there and lock them up? They're all fit to be tied.

He'd warned Artemis. From the very beginning he told her not to open up to anyone. Stay sharp, he said. If they start asking about the restaurant, just play dumb, change the subject. Be careful, he said, it's bad luck for them to be talking about us. Of course he was wasting his breath. He might as well have been talking to himself. Women. Sew up their mouths, their eyes, bind them hand and foot – they'll still find a way to talk.

And then it happened, what he'd feared. They all started chiming in with their two cents.

You should definitely make it a fish place.

Yeah, but just stick to the little ones, anchovies, sardines.

For sure. Who's going to spring for big fish these days?

I say make it one of those gourmet restaurants, or an ethnic place. That way you'll attract the best clientele, and tourists too.

Come on, man. You think they're going to serve Chinese food or something?

Why not? You see how many Chinese tourists we get these days. And they're here by Easter, before high season even starts.

Sure, but why would they come all the way from Shanghai just to eat Chinese food? Are you guys totally nuts?

Make it a mezze place. They're the only ones that stay open in winter, too.

Will you be open for lunch?

Where are you going to get your tables and chairs?

What kind of decor are you thinking?

Who's going to work the kitchen?

How about live music?

Will you serve coffee, too?

Are you looking for waiters?

Anyhow, you two are lucky, said Frankie, a wimp with a ponytail and earring who threw his own eighty-year-old grandfather out on the street so he could turn the family home into a bed and breakfast. There isn't too much paperwork in the restaurant business. We ran around for three years trying to get our permits.

I don't believe it, said Artemis. Three years?

He's not exaggerating, said Asi, the wimp's wife. Three whole years. The house is in a traditional settlement and pretty well preserved. The Ministry of Tourism, the tax bureau, fire inspectors, city planners, archaeologists – they bounced us back and forth like a ping pong ball. To this day, the thought of it makes my blood boil.

Not to mention all the expenses, and grease for the wheels, Frankie said.

Of course, said Asi. Not to mention all that.

And then there were the snitches, in the beginning, and the fines.

There was that, too.

Snitches? Artemis said. Who would snitch on you guys?

The other two looked at one another and laughed. Frankie tamped down the gauze on his forehead and poured a little whiskey in his glass and Stavros's. Then he turned away and swallowed a pill he had in his hand. Asi stopped laughing and nudged him with her elbow. She took Artemis's glass and filled it with wine. Her hand shook.

You poor thing, she said, wiping her eyes with a pinky finger. Seems to me you guys still haven't realized what it's like around here. Do you have any idea the kind of shit that goes on? The only thing we've got more of than squealers is rats. Really, who would snitch on us? You might as well ask who didn't. First about the septic tank, then about the sprinklers, then the solar panels on the roof – every week we had a new set of complaints to deal with, they were like a dog with a toy in its mouth. They even went online to register complaints, pretending to be customers, that the rooms smelled like mold, that they'd seen roaches or mice, that we stole their money or took stuff out of their suitcases – it was madness. Eventually they lost interest and stopped, but until then, we spit blood. I'm telling you, blood.

I'm not so sure, Frankie said. There might be even more squealers than rats. Either way, you should watch out.

Watch out for what? Artemis said, looking at Stavros, who was sitting there silently, head bowed. We're on good terms with everyone.

Maybe. Maybe you are on good terms with everyone, but everyone might not be on good terms with you. We were cool with everyone too, but apparently they weren't cool with us back. That's why I'm telling you to watch out.

Guys, what's going on? Artemis asked. What's that look for?

Tell them, Frankie said to Asi. Come on. Spit it out.

Let's just calm down, she told him. It's eleven and you guys are already on your second bottle. Calm down, OK?

Then she turned to Artemis and started to speak. She said that for a long time lots of people had an eye on the restaurant, and about once a year they would ask the German if he would sell, so they could turn it into a club or coffee shop, or knock it down and build some kind of lodging for tourists. Two or three years ago, rumor had it that the German finally decided to give it to that trigger-happy guy they call Jaguar, who owns half the places down by the water, but then he got cold feet, and ever since then Jaguar really had it in for him. And when he found out that the German rented the place to Artemis and Stavros, he hit the roof, you know how these things are, guys like that go apeshit if they don't get their way. I mean, he and his cousins were partners for years, and when they decided to split up the partnership a few years ago they almost ended up dueling with pistols in the street. And sure, you'll tell me those guys are dealing with millions, they've got everyone on the payroll, mayors, cops, tax officers, no one gives them any trouble. But the little guys? They're even worse, they'll sing like a canary for a handful of change. Didn't that sneak from Corinth go and set up his canteen down on the beach in Charos and within two days they'd torched the place? Didn't they beat those young guys almost to death down at Magou just for selling loukoumades and watermelon to tourists on the beach? And you think I could forget Astrinos, who left behind a wife and two kids? That poor guy. They drove him nuts, and he went and blew his brains out in the cave. Those bastards are the worst, guys like Xellinakis or the Ikariot, they've got no limits, no shame. That son of a bitch from Ikaria hung a banner outside the shacks to advertise his Russians and now all the dregs of humanity go and fuck girls their daughters' age and the fucking cops turn a blind eye whenever they pass by. They're all pieces of shit, all pimps and stool pigeons, the whole lot of them. Every single one, from first to last.

Artemis listened with her hand clamped tightly over her mouth as if there were something inside struggling to get out. She kept throwing glances at Stavros, who sat there rotating his glass with his hand and seemed to be listening only to the glin glin of ice cubes rattling.

I don't believe it, she said at last.

What part?

Any of it, Asi. Come on, that sort of thing can't be happening, it doesn't make any sense. There's so much tourism on the island. So many restaurants, cafés, tavernas. How did they all get built? There's no way. I don't believe it.

Don't fool yourself, girl. It's not 1990 anymore, or even 2000. It's a war zone out there. It's life or death. The fewer of us there are, the better. The guy next door isn't going to let you just waltz over and grab the food off his plate. Look at what's happening around you. You think the locals are all just thrilled we've shown up here? They're at each other's throats as it is – you think they're going to welcome us with open arms? I mean, why do you think they call us foreigners? You think that's a good sign?

Asi filled their glasses with wine and set the bottle back on the table.

Whatever, she said, I didn't say all that to scare you. We just want you to have your wits about you, to watch your backs. Come on, let's talk about something else, you look like you saw a ghost. Have some wine. You need some courage, girl. And don't be afraid of fear. Only the dead aren't afraid.

Is it true, though? Frankie said. What I heard about the prices. Are you really going to serve a set menu for ten euros?

For a minute no one spoke. Frankie looked at Artemis and Artemis looked at Asi, who was looking at Frankie as if she wanted to climb over the table and put out his eyes. Only Stavros was still staring at his glass, as if he'd made some bet with himself that he wouldn't look up until all the ice had melted.

We'll see, Artemis finally said. We haven't decided yet. We'll see, I don't know.

OK, Frankie said. But if you want my advice, I'd say you should think twice.

Why? Say we serve fifty people a night – fifty times

ten is five hundred. We'll cover the rent in a single day. What more do we need?

That's not how it works, Artemis. You're opening a business, not a soup kitchen. You can't just do whatever you want. You have to follow the system.

What system?

The system. It's like me renting a double room for twenty euros a night when everyone else in my category charges a hundred. That's not how things work. There's a system. There are cartels.

Come on, you guys are driving me crazy tonight, Artemis said. What are you talking about, Frankie? You're telling me there's an ouzeri cartel?

There are all kinds of cartels, everywhere. Greece has more cartels than Colombia, didn't you know? I mean, you can't buy potatoes for, I don't know, seventy cents a kilo and then pop them in the oven and sell a serving for a euro and a half if everyone else is charging three. You can't even charge the same amount for a serving of sardines, but put fifteen on the plate instead of eight. In Athens things are different, there are more people there, and more restaurants, so everyone does as they please. But that shit doesn't fly down here. Here you have to follow the system. Otherwise, you're asking for trouble. If the rats find out you're undercutting them, they're not going to let you just sit pretty on your branch. It's simple, really.

I don't know, Artemis said. So far, at least, nothing's happened. No one's bothered us.

And I hope no one does, said Frankie. But remember, these things are like earthquakes. You never know when they'll hit, and when they do, it's too late.

Come on, enough already, said Asi. Enough, I'm about ready to throw this fucking bottle out the window.

We want to do something different, Artemis said again. We have lots of plans.

Frankie shrugged his shoulders and raised his glass.

Okay, he said. Bon chance.

Stavros drained the rest of his whiskey, then stood up and reached for his coat.

Don't get mad, Stavrakos, Asi said. We're only telling you for your own good.

I'm not mad, Stavros said. I'm tired. Are you coming or should I go?

I'm coming, Artemis said. Go on, I'll be there in five minutes.

Stavros stopped in the doorway and looked at Frankie, who had collapsed face-up on the couch and was staring at the ceiling.

What happened to your head? he asked Frankie.

At the bed and breakfast, I was messing with some wires and fell off the ladder.

You know the story about Gagarin's scar?

Frankie raised his head and fumbled at the gauze on his forehead, giving Stavros a blank look.

Who the hell is Gagarin?

The Russian astronaut, Yuri Gagarin. After he became the first person to travel in space, he totally lost control, went the whole rock star route. Parties, women, vodka by the barrel, the whole deal. Well, at some point he's holed up in a hotel with some nurse, and his wife finds out, comes up to the room and starts hollering and pounding on the door, and Yuri panics, jumps off the balcony and lands on his head on the pavement. After that he had a scar on his forehead, right where yours is going to be, over the eyebrow. When people asked him about it afterward, he would tell some people that his daughter hit him with a rock, others that he fell off a ladder.

Frankie sat down on the sofa and shot a look at Asi, who was listening with her mouth hanging open.

What's all this shit, man? What does that have to do with anything?

Nothing, Stavros said. I just remembered. Anyhow, I'm off. Goodnight, or good morning, I guess.

At the front door he heard Asi shouting and slamming things on the table. He stood there for a minute, listening, then put on his coat and stepped out into the street.

———

He drinks a tall glass of tsikoudia and smokes two or three cigarettes, then pulls over a stool so he can climb up into the crawl space. The kite is way on the other side, leaning against the wall. It has colored horizontal stripes and a long tail and a string several meters long. He pushes down hard and lifts himself through the opening and, crouching on all fours, pulls the kite over and lets it fall onto the floor, its tail trailing after. Then, kneeling there, he thinks about cutting off a few meters of the string, tying one end to the ceiling beam and the other around his neck and jumping out of the crawl space – jumping through the opening, and there, in that small span between floor and hole, ending everything, everything ending for good, once and for all, forever.

A kite string tied to a ceiling beam.

He knows it's possible, he's heard stories. One guy tied his neck tie to a hook on the wall, another used his winter scarf and a heating pipe, someone even used a shoelace and a doorknob. Tie, shoelace, scarf – whatever's at hand.

A kite string tied to a ceiling beam.

Difficult, but not impossible.

Once and for all, forever.

Holding the ball of string he thinks how he'd like to have a foot in his brain, a steel foot wearing a steel boot so he could kick pain and bitterness far away, each time they came he could kick away betrayal, and despair, and bad people, harsh people, the kind of people who cut love to their own size and not to the size of love itself, people who say I love you on Monday and by Tuesday won't give you a second glance, say I can't live without you on Monday and by Tuesday say I can't stand you anymore, on Monday say we'll get through this together and by Tuesday say you have to stand on your own two feet, we all have to take responsibility for ourselves, on Monday say I want us to live together forever and by Tuesday say what do you mean I came into your life, fucked everything up, and now I'm leaving like nothing ever happened, what do you mean, I don't understand – you think I misled you or something? – people who say you're my forever person on Monday and by Tuesday say you're getting too clingy, you're asking too much, don't text me anymore, don't call, people who laugh with all their heart while yours drips blood, who watch TV calmly at night until they fall asleep without a care in the world, while you stare through the window at the darkness and feel that darkness swallowing you up, people who forget you overnight and spend their days and nights with friends in cafés and bars, while you remember everything – each moment, each word, each kiss, each night, each day – you remember each whisper, each cry, each embrace, each smile, each laugh, you remember, remember, remember, and you struggle, your hands dipped in blood, your heart soaked in blood, your eyes soaked in clear, crystalline blood, you struggle, every hour, every moment, every morning, every night, to eradicate everything you remember from your body and heart and mind, to uproot everything your body and heart and mind remember, you struggle to douse with blood the blaze that consumes you, you struggle not to remember, you struggle to forget the sweetness in those eyes that gazed into your eyes, the taste of that other mouth when it kissed yours, the smell of that other body tangled with yours, you struggle not to remember, to not remember. You struggle to learn to not remember. And you're afraid. You're afraid you won't manage, afraid that one day you won't be able to bear it anymore and you'll make the biggest mistake, you'll close your eyes and take a deep breath and take out your phone and call, or even worse, you'll go and stand outside her house, outside his house, and it'll be night and cold and raining and you'll stand there for hours in the rain and cold, waiting, smoking, shaking, your eyes shattered, your heart shattered, your mind shattered, you'll wait and wait until you see her coming, until you see him coming, and then you'll toss your cigarette onto the harsh wet pavement and drag yourself over to her, over to him – and you know you're capable of falling to your knees and crawling to kneel at her feet, at his feet – and you'll say in your shattered voice, please, I'm begging you, listen to me, just listen for a minute, just one minute, I love you, I don't care if I've lost my sense of self, all that matters is that I'm losing you, I love you, just give me a chance to show you how much I love you, how much I loved you, how much I'll love you still, I'm begging you, I don't care that I'm on my knees, I don't care that I'm begging, just give me a chance, you can't have forgotten it all, you can't already have forgotten the nights we spent together, the Friday afternoons, that Tuesday when I bought you those sunglasses, the Saturday we went to the Hondos Center and you bought me perfume and afterward I gave you twenty cents so it wouldn't bring bad luck, you can't have forgotten, you can't have forgotten the Sunday afternoon when you made pasta with shrimp, peppers, and feta and you primped and preened, so proud of how well it turned out and I said, this isn't pasta with shrimp, it's pasta with primp, and we laughed and went to bed, leaving the food on the table, and then took a shower together and splashed water in one another's eyes and laughed some more and finally ate and drank the bottle of wine I brought and the profiteroles for dessert, you can't not remember, just give me a chance, I love you more than I've ever loved in my life, more than I'll ever love again, don't leave, please, don't leave me. That's what you'll say, on your knees, and then you'll raise your eyes and see the most terrible thing a person can ever see, a crippled person, a kneeling person in love – an unsmiling, harsh, tight face, which you thought until now was a mask hiding the pain, but just now you realize, shaking all over, that what you thought was a mask is the actual face of the person you love, the person you thought loved you, and you'll wonder for a moment, the briefest moment, how it's possible, how on earth the eyes that once dripped such sweetness as they gazed at you are the same eyes that are looking at you tonight so impassively, so indifferently – and then, shaking even harder, on your knees, you'll hear the most terrible thing a crippled, kneeling person in love can hear.

I told you, it's over. What precisely don't you understand? It's over, we're over. O-ver.

Everything.

Over.

The little mermaid is still perched on her rock, propped on one arm, legs bent to the side, still staring out to sea, hair gathered so the wind won't muss it — the little mermaid stares out at the sea, and she isn't so little anymore, or a mermaid, either.

Before he gets out of the car, she turns and looks his way, and when he opens the trunk and pulls out the kite she smiles and gets to her feet and stands on the rock with her arms stretched out to either side, her face glowing as if suddenly lit by an invisible spotlight. Stavros holds the kite in one hand and the multi-colored tail in the other, and as he walks toward her he wonders if that smile is for him or the kite or something else altogether. The sky has cleared, the sun is shining as strong as two suns together, and a sweet breeze blows from the north, making the waves shiver.

Everyone will think we're nuts, he calls to her, setting the kite down on the pebbles of the beach and carefully laying out the tail so it doesn't get tangled. Kites are for Clean Monday. No one flies kites in July. That's it, they've lost it, they'll say.

Artemis comes over carrying the little lamps in one hand and the life preserver with the message welcoming mermaids in the other. She stands and looks at Stavros, her head cocked to one side.

Yes, Artemis, don't worry. It's fine. I didn't forget.

He pulls the corkscrew out of his back pocket and hands it to her and she twists it into the cork, then puts the bottle between thighs blackened by ash and tugs until the cork comes out with a plop. She sniffs the wine, then takes a long swig and hands the bottle to Stavros.

How is it?

Nice. Smoky.

They light cigarettes and drink the wine standing up, there beside a restaurant destroyed by fire, staring silently out to sea, listening to the sea, smelling the sea, not talking. In the distance the other islands look white in the sunlight, like reflections, mirages of islands that once were but no longer are.

Can you cut a bit off the string? she asks.

Why?

Can you? I have an idea.

Another idea?

About ten centimeters. Or a bit longer.

He pulls the switchblade from his boot and folds the string over and cuts where Artemis tells him to.

Cut off another piece.

What's going on?

Just cut it. You'll see. Great. Now tie the string to the kite. And straighten the tail.

Artemis.

Tie it tightly, so it doesn't fall off. And make sure the tail doesn't get tangled.

Come on, Artemis, you must be joking. You really want us to fly a kite? They'll think we're –

Okay, I'll hold it and you run. Got it? Hold on, just a sec. Do you have gloves?

I don't need gloves.

Just put on the gloves. Otherwise the string will cut your hands. You remember what happened during Carnival.

No, I don't remember. I don't want to remember anything.

Fine. Then put on the gloves without remembering.

Artemis grabs the kite by either side and slowly walks backward, careful not to step on the tail. She goes about thirty meters off and stops. The wind is stronger now, and as she lifts her hands into the air the kite shudders, then rights itself, like a living creature that's been held hostage for a long time and is struggling to break free.

Ready?

No.

On three. One, two, three. Go! Run! Run!

Looking backward, running forward, Stavros grips the string in his gloved hands, tightly, jerking it now and again to make the kite take off, though for now it keeps rising and falling, as if it were about to crash into the earth – Stavros looks backward and runs forward, hearing Artemis cheer him on, and now the kite rises higher, balancing in the air, dancing and twirling, a captive creature longing to be free, longing for the string to break, to escape for good, once and for all, forever. Then he stops running and looks up, breathing hard, sweating, and sees the kite hovering high above his head, a small trembling sign, colorfully dissonant against the blinding blue of the sky.

Artemis comes over, holding the lanterns, the pieces of string, and the orange life preserver. The sweat has become one with the smudges on her face and she looks like a woman who's been crying black tears. But she's laughing. She's laughing, sweaty and out of breath, her eyes like two blue planets, twin planets made of water, looking out from a distance of millions of miles into space.

See? You see? I was right. See how high it went?

Stavros takes the glove off his right hand and gives it to her to wear. They hold the string together, free hands raised to keep the sunlight from blinding them, feeling the kite pull at every sudden gust of wind up high, which is the only sign that the kite is still tied to the string, because they can't even see it anymore, it's blended into the sky, nowhere to be seen.

Find a rock, Artemis says. A big one.

Another idea?

You'll see. Come on, it has to be big.

He carries a rock over and wraps the kite string around it several times. Artemis kneels down and ties one of the pieces of string to the life preserver. Then she stands back up and tells him to lower the kite string very slowly, until it's about ten meters off the ground.

Can you tell me what you're trying to do?

Be patient. Bring it down carefully. Gently, so nothing breaks.

Stavros grabs the string from where it's tied to the rock and starts to pull it down, walking forward until he reaches the curve in the road.

Now what?

Wait. I'm coming.

Artemis comes over and ties the string with the life preserver to the string of the kite. She tells Stavros to walk a little further. She follows him, and when he stops, she ties the second length of string in the middle, affixes it tightly to the kite string, and then ties one of the little lanterns to each end.

Okay. Now let it go. Slowly. Be careful.

It can't bear the weight.

Let it go, I'm telling you.

And I'm telling you it's too much. The kite will come crashing down. It'll drop down like a bullet. You'll see.

Nothing's going to happen. Let it go.

Fine. You'll see. Just don't go yelling at me afterwards. Don't take it out on me. I warned you.

Stavros closes his eyes, slowly lets the kite go from his hand, and when he opens his eyes again he sees the life preserver and lanterns jolting suddenly into the air, twisting for a moment and then hanging almost motionless, high up, ten or fifteen meters above the earth, as if suspended from nothing at all, as if they had started falling from the sky and then for some mysterious, magical reason, suddenly stopped falling and stayed there hovering in nothingness.

He waits. He holds his breath. With his hands above his head to block out the sun, he waits to see the string loosen and billow out wide, and then to see the kite falling, twisting with dizzying speed from up high and crashing into the earth like a bird that's been shot.

He waits. He waits with squinted eyes, holding his breath, listening to his heart beat as it had earlier, back at home, when he eyeballed the distance between the crawl space and the floor, or like today and yesterday, when he walked through the charred remains, or like the day before yesterday, when he watched helplessly as flames devoured the restaurant, or the day he spent packing their suitcases for the island, or the afternoon when he'd shoved the things from his office into plastic bags, or that night in December when, kneeling on the pavement, he saw and heard the most terrible thing a person can see and hear, a crippled, kneeling person in love.

Why are we doing this now? he asks. What does it mean? Why were you so intent on us flying a kite now, in the middle of July?

I don't know, Artemis said. Maybe because we've never done it before. And because it's something that's ours.

They watch as the lanterns and the life preserver spin gently in the air and then Artemis puts her arm around his shoulder and pulls him to her forcefully, like a man.

See? Nothing happened. Now let's go and sit on the rocks. We've still got another bottle.

—∞—

The string was invisible in the blinding sunlight. The lanterns and life preserver seemed to be floating in midair, dangling from nothingness over nothingness. Every so often the wind died down, and the lanterns would bump against one another, jingling in a strange, almost comforting way in the deserted landscape. Then someone passed by in a pickup truck and saw the lanterns and life preserver way up high, and slowed down and stuck his head out the window and looked at them, his mouth hanging open. He drove a little further and then stopped. He put the truck in reverse and came back and stared up at the sky, scratching his jaw. He looked around and when he saw Artemis and Stavros he seemed to realize something was going on, but he didn't know what. Then he stepped on the gas and drove off, honking the horn several times.

Later others passed by. They all stopped to take it in: two lanterns and a life preserver twirling in midair, dangling from nothingness over nothingness. An old woman made the sign of the cross. A kid on a motorbike took out his cell phone and snapped a few photos.

Artemis laughed. She curled up in Stavros's arms and kissed him. Her lips were red from the wine but didn't taste like anything burnt.

What are we going to do? he asked her.

Want to stay here? We can watch the moon rise. I think it's a full moon tonight.

I meant what are we going to do about this, Stavros said, pointing behind them. What are we going to do? We're ruined. All that money down the drain. What are we going to do now? How will we live? And what about the German? How can –

She put her fingers to his lips, which were also red with wine, and rubbed them hard.

We'll make a new start, she said.

Don't talk to me like that, OK? Don't talk to me like we're in some Hollywood movie. Everything's going to be fine and think positive and all that bullshit.

We'll make a new start, she said. That's what we'll do. We'll figure out how. We have no choice.

We already made our start. And now it's ash. Turn around and look. Look what happened to your new start. It's ash now. Just look. Look.

Artemis ran her fingers through his hair, stroked his ears, pinched his jaw.

The beginning is never behind us, she said. The beginning is always ahead.

Oh, great, now you're trotting out the Coelho-Bucay-Yalom shit. That's just great.

The beginning is always ahead. Say it.

Leave me alone, okay?

Say it. The beginning is always ahead.

I'm not saying anything.

Say it.

No.

Say it, please. Why won't you? Don't you love me anymore?

She looked him in the eyes. The liquid in hers had started to tremble.

Fine, don't get all bent out of shape. I'll say it.

Say it.

I said it on the inside.

Say it out loud. I want to hear it.

The beginning is always ahead, fuck all those fucking rats, fuck them.

His eyes burned. He rubbed them with his thumbs, looked out at the sea, and then turned to Artemis.

The beginning is always ahead, he said.

She leaned over and kissed him. Her lips were swollen, black with dried wine. Her tongue slipped slowly into his mouth, curled, stretched, then pulled back out again. She wrapped her arms around his head, sank her fingers into his hair, and pulled, hard.

I've never betrayed you, she said. Never. Remember that.

She shoved herself between his legs and with a sudden movement pulled up his shirt and started to kiss his chest. She squeezed his nipples, licked them, bit them, sank her nails into his back. Laughing, she pulled at a hair that had stuck to her lips and then bent down lower, licked his belly, stuck her tongue in his belly button, loosened his belt. Looking straight into his eyes, she took him in her hands and then in her mouth, licked him all over from the base to the head, then climbed onto him, pulled her panties aside and put him inside her, squeezing tightly, moaning, her head on his shoulder. Stavros looked down at the part weaving through her hair like a thin little adder and then closed his eyes and wondered, yet again, for the thousandth time, how many nipples she had licked, how many belts she had loosened, how many other men she had ridden like this. He stayed almost entirely still while Artemis bucked on top of him, and when she pulled herself off, his sperm leapt like a tiny white snake onto her belly.

But I betrayed you, he almost said – only yet again, he held his tongue.

He looked at her parted lips, which were still trembling, then wiped his own and took a swig of wine to wash the bitter taste from his mouth. Night was falling. The sea had begun to fill with shadows, the shadows of invisible things. Two crows flew cawing over their heads and disappeared in the direction of the sunset. The wind had died down, but every so often they could hear the jingling of the lanterns hanging from the string of the kite. The air here didn't smell burnt anymore. He closed his eyes and covered his face with his hands. They smelled like saltwater and Artemis and something else.

They're circles, he said.

Artemis looked at him, holding a swig of wine in her mouth, then swallowed and passed the bottle back to him.

What did you say?

Rainbows. They're not curved, they're circles.

Really? How can that be?

I don't know. I don't remember. Something about the sun and the horizon.

She took his hands in hers, then leaned to the side and snuggled into his embrace, looking out at the sea.

So what we're seeing is half the circle, she said.

Yes.

And the other half? Do you think we'll ever see it?

I don't know. Maybe.

That's nice. That's a nice thought.

She closed her eyes and when she opened them again she turned to look at the lanterns and life preserver, which now, in the violet light of dusk, looked more magical than ever. All sorts of things passed through her mind, but she didn't cry.

I'm hurting so much, she said, looking straight ahead, as if she were talking to the sea.

I know, said Stavros.

Most of all because I don't hate this country. I can't. It's like my mother, that's what I sometimes think. I could never really communicate with her, we couldn't talk for more than five minutes without fighting, and at times she scared me or drove me crazy, but I couldn't ever hate her. I can't hate this country. Even if I wanted to, I never could. Never. There's no way.

Stavros lowered his eyes and looked at the part in her hair. He hesitated for a moment and then reached out a finger and traced the straight line, his finger on her skin, which was warm and sweaty.

She raised her head and looked at him, smiling, then suddenly jolted upright in his arms and started clapping.

So, I just had an idea.

And you can unhave it again just as fast. I'm not going anywhere, or cutting anything, or carrying anything. You've had enough ideas for one day.

Listen, we'll make it a kind of tradition. We'll come here on this day each July and fly a kite. What do you think? It's a good idea, right? We'll tell the others in the neighborhood, too, and we'll all come here and fly kites. And each one of us will tie something to the string and let it hang in the air, like we did with the lanterns and life preserver. And we'll all sit together with our food and our wine and look up at the sky for hours. And then we'll cut the strings and let the kites and the objects leave, let the wind take them, let them disappear. What do you think? Won't it be nice?

Stavros took out two cigarettes, lit them both and handed her one. They smoked, listening to the waves, smelling the salt spray, looking at the lights from the other islands in the distance, the lights on the ships passing by on the open sea, the lights of the fishing boats casting out nets or pulling them up again, so many lights flickering in the half dark.

We'll turn it into a tradition, Artemis said. If we have to live here, we need to come up with some new traditions, our own traditions. That's what we have to do.

He looked at her and started to speak, then stopped. He licked his thumb and rubbed at a sooty fingerprint on her forehead. From the direction of the restaurant, behind them, they heard a loud sound like something tumbling to the ground. He felt the hairs on the back of his neck rising like needles pulled by an enormous magnet, but didn't turn around to look.

He reached out a hand and pointed at the lanterns.

Do you want to –

Yes, Artemis said. Do you?

They stood up and walked over to the rock that was anchoring the string. For a while they watched the two lanterns and life preserver twisting in the air and then Stavros kneeled down and pulled the switchblade out of his boot.

I wish we could do that, Artemis said. I wish we could tie ourselves to a string and get up that high and look down on the world from up there. Can you imagine? Wouldn't it be nice?

I don't know. It depends. Would they cut our string afterward or not?

She mussed his hair, laughing, then kneeled beside him and together they held the string.

Ready?

Artemis looked at his hands, his lips, his eyes, blurry and red, the whites of the eyes shot through with tiny bloody threads. For a moment it seemed – she was certain – that she could hear his eyelids blinking, the blood rushing through his veins.

You know, she said, there's no secret to any of it. Life needs to live. That's all. There's no secret.

Stavros folded the string just above the rock and sliced it with a sudden movement. The string slipped through his hands and flew up high. They stood and watched, arm in arm, as the lanterns and life preserver soared slowly to the west, toward the setting sun, until all three disappeared from sight, just as the kite had hours earlier.

On that side of the island the wind rarely blew from the east. It might never have blown like that before, and might never again. They talked about it for a while, later, when they were sitting once more on the rocks, and agreed they didn't care at all. They didn't give a damn. It didn't bother them one bit.

Because that night the wind was blowing from the east, for sure.

When the north wind blows on this island, it tears down everything in its path. But we've never seen anything like what happened today. The school bus set off from town to go and pick up the kids from Antilalos and the other villages, and on the straightaway we call the Doors, the wind knocked it right off the road and it fell on the rocks. All the way down, over the cliff. Can you believe it? Nothing like it ever happened before. Luckily the driver survived, but just imagine if the kids had been in there.

Well.

What do you mean, well?

If that isn't a sign, what is?

My father is doing his evening exercises. He's passed a length of red string between the toes of his left foot and keeps pulling it upwards with his hand, counting from one to seventy-seven. He pauses for a while, wiggles his toes like someone's tickling him, then starts all over again. It's a new trick, and I have to keep an eye on it all, because you can't leave him alone with so much as a bit of thread, much less a whole ball of string.

It's true, he says. When the French and the Germans go on about radon and becquerels, you stand there listening like idiots. When Yiannis the Baptized by Stroke opens his mouth, not one of you pays any attention. Doubting Thomases, every last one. Speaking of which, this afternoon I'd like you to gather all the illiterate fools in the town square and tell them that we put our finger on the heart of the matter, not in it. We get down to brass tacks, not on brass tacks. On, not in – and to, not on. Illiterate clods, the whole lot of them. And at church on Sunday, tell that drunken mess of a priest, Babajim, to get rid of the icon of the Holy Trinity that shows God with white hair and a beard, like a little old man with great-grandkids running around, because we Orthodox only paint what we've seen, and since we've never seen God, we shouldn't paint him. And the icon of Saint Marina, the one that shows her holding the devil by his horns, he should put that one away, too, this isn't Hollywood, there's no need for us to go around showing devils and horns and all that, we only paint things that have substance, and the devil, evil itself, is unsubstantial. Mind you, unsubstantial, *not nonexistent. Evil exists, but it doesn't have substance, because only the things God created have substance, and God didn't create devils, he created angels – even if some of them later decided to become devils. Tell him that. Enough already with the heathens and false theologizers, tell him that. Enough already. Enough is enough, ça suffit, rien ne va plus, ze maspik. Otherwise I might get it into my head to go down there one day and cart away those icons myself.*

He sighs up at the ceiling, then starts counting again under his breath, pulling the string up and down.

Swiss, I say.

He looks at me sideways, wrinkling his left eyebrow, still counting.

The seismologists, I say. They're not French and German. They're Swiss and German.

What was I thinking? In seconds flat his face is bright red, he lets the string drop from his hand and starts kicking at the covers with his left foot, struggling to turn toward me. What was I thinking, opening my mouth? A rookie mistake, and a big one.

Is that how far we've sunk? His voice wavers, his mouth even more twisted than before. Have we sunk this far, that a slip of a girl like you would mock her sick father?

Well, that's as sure a sign as any. It's a black day today, black as a jackdaw. In the morning the school bus plunges over a cliff, at night a daughter mocks her father. And hark, a great sign was seen in the heavens, of a daughter mocking her father. Other signs won't be far behind. Soon enough you'll see fish writhing on dry land like the eyelids of a man having a bad dream. And you'll see living people fighting around the body of a dead one, who was young, handsome, and persecuted, like Christ. Any day now, so prepare yourself. All that's coming, too, soon enough. And then you'll believe me. But it'll be too late, far too late.

He closes his eyes and falls back onto the pillow. He's covered in sweat but won't let me wipe him down, he shakes his head right and left, moans, hits himself like he does when it's time for me to give him his Duphalac.

And then he sits up again in bed and grabs me by the arm and pulls me toward him.

Watch out, he whispers. Listen carefully, when you talk to the priest on Sunday about the icons, make sure there's no one else around.

OK, I say. I'll make sure.

That's a good girl. I don't want anyone to find out your father believes in God. Because these days when you say you believe in God, everyone looks at you as if you've said you invite little girls into your living room every night and give them candies and lollipops and dandle them on your knee. So be careful. Not for my sake but for yours. I don't want Dawkins, Hitchens, and that other guy, the French one, what's his name, Onfray, to see you in the street and to laugh and say, there goes the daughter of Yiannis, who believes in God. So be careful.

OK, I got it, I say.

And tonight he'll wake me up again, shouting to me from his room, and he'll tell me not to stay up all night staring out the window at the stars and the clouds, because I have an early morning tomorrow, I have work to do.

First thing in the morning, he'll say, you're going to go and take some money out of the bank and give it to that fool of a mayor to buy a new bus. And tell him that from now on I'll ride with the kids to school – they won't have anything to fear. Even if the wind is blowing at hurricane force, I'll be with them on the bus, there won't be anything to fear. Just look here, he'll say, pulling up the sleeve of his pajamas. Look here, he'll say, and flex his left arm, sticking his jaw out and clenching his teeth. Just look at that muscle, like a mouse under the skin.

More rat than mouse, really. Nothing at all to fear. I'll be there.

We have to save the children, he'll tell me. The children have to be there when the end comes, the children have to see the end, they have to be there when the end comes.

The children, the end.

The end, he'll say, whispering in the dark.

The end.